MR. HOLLYWOOD'S SECRET

ADORA CROOKS

NICO

My boyfriend lies in bed beside me, sweat-slicked, panting, and frustrated.

I try to reason with him. "It happens to plenty of guys—"

"If the next words out of your mouth are *at your age*, I'm going to kill you."

Eric North is, objectively, a vision. At forty-five, he has a chiseled body that men *half* his age would be envious of. Top that off with a grizzled beard, dazzling blue eyes, and thick hair that is going silver in all the right ways, it's not hard to see why the camera loves him.

Or why I love him. Why I've been *in* love with him for the past five years.

He has a soft side to him. Underneath that rugged, steely exterior.

Unfortunately, Eric is embarrassed right now, and he has all of his walls up. There is no grappling hook I can use to climb walls that high.

I try, regardless. I slip my hand over his chest, comforting.

"You've been pushing yourself too hard," I reassure him. "The movie. The stress."

He moves away from my hand and sits up. He leans back

against the hard oak of our headboard. "The only one who's been pushing me is my agent," he says. "She won't let up about this fiancée bullshit."

I press my lips together. This topic of conversation has been the source of grunting and growling from Eric for weeks.

You see, Eric, the action-movie star, Hollywood's favorite leading man, has one very large secret...

Me.

Five years we've been dating. Three, we've been living together. And still, no one outside of our close-knit group of friends and family knows about us. No one knows he's gay.

I sit up beside him. "Do you want to talk about it?"

Coaxing Eric out of his shell is a nearly impossible task. However, every now and then, if you ask in just the right way, he'll give in. "She keeps hounding me. She wants to set me up with a fake fiancée for the convention. She says it will be good for the PR run."

"Is that what you *want* to do?" I ask.

Those blue eyes go sharp as knives. "Obviously not."

I exhale a deep breath. "Alright. I have...an idea. Well. Less of an idea and more of a person."

His lips draw into a thin line. "What did you have in mind?"

* * *

Eric and I live in a two-story house in San Marino, Los Angeles.

It's a Mediterranean-style house with a red tile roof, ivy that climbs the exterior walls, and large, high-archway doors. Inside are hardwood floors, Vanguardia paintings on the walls, ceremonial masks from Mexico, and abstract sculptures cluttered around our immense living room. We're closed off from the world, behind a private gate and giant hedges.

The house's personality is mostly mine; when I moved in, it immediately became clear that Eric hadn't moved a stick of furniture since he walked the house with his Realtor and said, "I'll take it." At one point, I'd pointed to a piece of tape over one of the light switches in the kitchen and asked him what it was there for. He'd just shrugged and informed me it'd always been there.

I couldn't let that stand—to the point where I tore into the wall and nearly electrocuted myself not once, but twice to find the source of the phantom switch.

And that, truly, is us in a nutshell.

Eric would rather ignore a problem than change it (even if it is for his own good).

I, meanwhile, am incapable of leaving a problem unsolved (even if it is to my own detriment).

My favorite part of the house is out back, through the french doors, where it exits to a sparkling pool, a spa Jacuzzi, and an outdoor kitchen. Large palm trees hang over a long wooden table and ivy-covered awning, which is where we often host intimate dinner parties for our small circle of friends who *know*.

I come here to write and when I need an escape.

Like now. I want to be alone for the phone call I'm about to make.

I sit on the edge of the pool, dip my bare toes in the water, and call Chrys Hudson.

We went to college together and spent most of that time utterly inseparable, but we haven't spoken in years—save the occasional "like" on each other's posts or mild banter through Facebook comments. I prepare myself for an awkward conversation, but as soon as the phone stops ringing, the first thing I hear is "Nico fucking Ortega, this better not be a butt dial."

2

CHRYS

I'm in the middle of a meeting with my agent when Nico calls.

The Bartlett Agency operates out of a small, hole-in-the-wall cement building on the outskirts of LA, right across the street from a Taco Bell. There's a glass door that always seems to have a crack in it, a waiting room with plastic chairs, and a desk that constantly rotates through blonde, buxom secretaries.

The office I'm sitting in is a cramped space with a bookshelf filled with script binders, B-list movie posters on the wall, and an ornate desk.

Felix the Cat watches me from above, his eyes and tail swishing back and forth with each tick of the second hand on his belly.

My agent, Roger Barlett, thinks the cat clock is hip. Vintage. He thinks it makes him quirky and authentic. But a cat clock isn't a personality.

It's just a clock. And, frankly, it's unnerving, and it puts me on edge every time I sit in his office. I fiddle with the hem of my dress. I feel exposed here, and I wish I'd worn something that goes down to my ankles instead of my knees.

Roger sits across from me on a worn, plush purple couch I've come to loathe. He's a tall man with a widow's peak and a mustache that he clearly loves more than he loves his own grandmother. He has an open script in his hands, and he's gripping it like it's the Holy Grail.

"I mean, it's like this part was written for you," he says.

"That's great!" I try to sound enthusiastic.

"It is," he agrees. He pets his mustache with his thumb and forefinger. "Except…"

Here we go.

"Well, the caliber of the people involved in this project… they're up there, you know? But, good news for you, I *know* the casting director. Personally. We go way back."

This is a common story for him. *We go way back* is his favorite phrase. I've come to take everything he says with a grain of salt. So far, the only parts he's managed to book for me are a couple of commercials and unnamed characters on TV shows.

Not that I'm complaining. At least I'm booking *something*.

LA is swarming with redheaded, starry-eyed hopefuls just like me. I'll take what I can get.

"Cool." I smile. "Sounds like a match."

"Yes." He nods. He stares at me. He's waiting.

Dear God, don't make me say it.

This is the dance we do. I want the roles. He wants *something else* from me.

I pull on a practiced smile. "What do you need from me?"

I've said the right thing. A smirk curls the edge of his mouth, and he runs his hand up his thigh. "Well…I think you know the answer to that."

My stomach churns. Bile in my throat.

This is what they didn't teach you in acting school.

How to Avoid Unwanted Advances by Your Agent 101.

I'd take that class in a heartbeat, now.

Felix watches us from above, his siltted eyes leering.

Suddenly, my pocket starts vibrating.

Thank God.

I take out my phone quickly and check the caller ID.

Nico? I haven't spoken to him in years.

But right now, he's saving my dignity.

I lift the phone and give it a shake. "Sorry, I've got to take this—one second."

Roger's expression goes sour. "Opportunity won't wait forever."

Asshole.

I step outside his office building to take the call. Even with the exhaust from the nearby highway, the air smells better out here.

"Nico fucking Ortega," I answer. "This better not be a butt dial."

He laughs. The sound is achingly familiar, and immediately, I'm nostalgic. My nerves, which feel like a box of pins rattling around on top of a washing machine, immediately relax at the sound of his voice.

"Chrys fucking Hudson," he responds, "it's been much too long."

We fall into easy conversation. He asks all of the polite questions one asks after too many years have gone by—how am I doing? Have I been in any shows lately? Married? Boyfriend? Kids?

I give him the CliffsNotes version of the last ten years of my life: I'm doing alright, nothing but the forever grind of auditions. No boyfriends at the moment (or for years, if we're being honest), only a roommate and a shoe-box apartment and our shared cat.

We reminisce: our wild, wonderful college years. I'm thirty now and feel far older than I should, but talking to Nico takes me back.

"This is going to sound crazy," Nico says, "but do you

remember that time you took me to your parents for Thanksgiving?"

I laugh. "Uh, how could I forget? We pretended you were my boyfriend. Really threw them through a loop."

We also did...uh...*non-pretend boyfriend and girlfriend* stuff on that trip, but neither of us mentions it now.

The memory does send a ripple of warmth through me, and I can't tell if it's his honey-smooth voice or the hot LA sun that makes me sweat.

"Right," Nico continues. "And when we came back...you said that you owed me. And if I ever needed a favor, no matter what, I could cash it in."

"I think I can see where this is going...what's the favor?"

On the other end, I hear Nico take a deep breath.

"Well," he says, "I need you to marry my boyfriend."

ERIC

*M*onica clicks the door shut.

"She's cute," she says, examining Chrys' headshot, "likable. A little homey, but people go for that these days. Girl-next-door vibes. The tabloids will love her. I can see why you picked her."

"I didn't pick her. Nico did."

I'm folded onto my agent's blue suede couch, fingers pressed to the side of my head.

Everything hurts these days. My skull. My back. My heart.

Monica slides the headshot onto the glass coffee table between us. "Whatever the case, she's not a bad candidate. Don't you think?"

"Mm."

Monica folds her arms over her chest. "How long have I been your agent?"

"Long."

"So I'm going to tell you the truth because someone has to. Listen, Eric. You're forty-five. If you keep on your exercise regimen, you have maybe three more years of leading

8

man left in you. After that, it's commercials for Viagra and Hallmark films."

I sneer, indignant.

"Don't believe me? Ask Roger Moore."

I rub my hand over my knee. "I thought the point of this movie was to open the conversation."

The movie I'm promoting—*Catch & Kill*—is different from my action movies in the past for one reason. My main character, who is a bit of a James Bond-style spy, sleeps around indiscriminately to get the information he needs. In this film, one of his targets happens to be a man—my co-star, Raul Díaz. The scene is treated like any other; it's sexy, it's dangerous. The kiss is closed mouth, the pants stay on, but the implication is further than any other box-office-busting action movie has gone before.

It's what drew me to the part. Only now that I've opened up a little bit on camera, I feel my agent pushing me further back into my shell.

She sighs and sits down across from me. "It is," she tells me. "And you have. This movie will help open a dialogue and pave the way for movies to come. Which is why we have to be careful about how we handle this. We don't want to do too much all at once."

"Paving the way is great for everyone who comes after," I tell her. "Not so much for me."

"Sacrifices we have to make. Look, you are what flyover states call a *silver fox*. So milk it while you can. Don't throw your career away on something stupid."

Something stupid. The words echo in my head.

Nico isn't something stupid, I want to tell her.

Love isn't something stupid. The words hang on my lips.

But the fear of losing everything I've worked so hard for glues my tongue to the roof of my mouth, and I hate myself for it.

9

I tap my fingertips on the headshot and nudge it toward Monica.

"Just tell me what to do," I say.

NICO

*I*t's Eric's last meal.

His last meal as a gay man, anyway. Tomorrow, he'll go to Paris for a conference and then hop across two more cities for interviews with his fake fiancée on his arm. Tomorrow, he'll be Eric North, the most heterosexual man in Hollywood.

He's certainly eating as though it's his last meal. And drinking. I haven't been counting—I try not to count; best not to micromanage these things—but I'm pretty sure he polished off two very expensive bottles of pinot noir all on his own.

The night drags on, his sentences begin to slur, and one by one, our guests politely bow out before things get ugly. All but one.

"Do you need a hand with that?"

I glance up from my spot at the sink. Alex, our lingering friend, rolls up the sleeves of his button-up.

"No," I tell him, "but since you made the mistake of volunteering, you're welcome to dry."

Alex steps in beside me, takes the dish towel, and starts patting the dishes dry as I pass them over. He's a trans man, and he's butterflied quite beautifully, with bulky biceps, a handsome beard, and a couple of facial accessories: a bottom lip piercing and eyebrow ring. Long before I met Eric, Alex and I dated for a couple of months. I've never dated on a binary—men, women, and everyone in between...it doesn't matter how you identify, as far as I'm concerned, as long as the connection is there. Alex and I shared a warm, placid relationship and ended on good terms.

Eric only got prickly about me being friends with an ex once. He can get possessive, and it came out in a bad flare. "I don't know that I like the idea of eating across from a guy who's seen you naked," Eric had said.

"Well," I'd responded, "I don't like the idea of you flirting with your co-stars for the camera, but I suppose we both have to make sacrifices."

He'd shut up about it after that.

Our relationship only works as long as we have rules—outlined and carefully observed. I respect his boundaries: I never ask for more than he can give. He, in turn, respects mine: he doesn't get to tell me who to be friends with.

This is the precarious structure that keeps our house of cards upright.

"Eric is sloshed," Alex comments as he stacks dishes in the rack.

"I've noticed."

"How do you feel about it?"

"He's built like a horse. He'll metabolize it soon enough."

"No—I mean the woman."

Ah. *The woman.* As though she is some evil force to be reckoned with. She-who-must-not-be-named.

"Chrys. I think they're a good match." Scrub, scrub, scrub. Steak sauce refuses to leave the plate. "We were friends in college. She's fun. Who knows, maybe she'll even loosen him up."

Alex lets out a heavy sigh. "How much longer is he going to put you through this?"

I feel my bones stiffen. How many times have we had this conversation? "It's not easy for him, either."

"No. It's not good for *either* of you," Alex presses. "It's toxic to deny who you are. I should know. He's miserable. You're miserable. Something's got to give."

"Alex." I turn off the faucet, forcing him to look at me. "Yes. The situation is complicated. But Eric loves me. Deeply. And I love him. No matter what, we have that."

"Is that enough?" Alex asks.

Before I have time to respond, the porch door slides open. Eric's bare feet slap on the tiled floors. "What's going on here?" he asks. As though we're building *bombs* or something.

"Dishes," I respond. "Would you like to help?"

Alex dries his hands off on the dish towel. "It's getting late. I should head out."

I tell him to drive safe. We embrace briefly, and he clasps Eric on the shoulder. I hear the front door open and close behind him. I turn back to the sink, rinsing off the last plate. Out of the corner of my eye, I see Eric reach up to grab a glass from the top shelf. His shirt slides up as he does, and I can't help but sneak a peak of his bare midriff. The well-defined lines of his abdomen. That perfect V steaming from the loose fit of his pants across hips.

I don't normally consider myself shallow, but he is proof that we are all sculpted in the image of the gods. He is molded after Ares, maybe, the god of war and mischief.

He tilts the glass to the filter on our fridge and fills it with water. He isn't as young as he used to be; his hangover will level him tomorrow if he doesn't take care of it now.

"Did you have fun tonight?" I ask.

"Mmhm." He drains the cup.

I'm not a proponent of getting sloppy drunk, but there is something nice about the way he looks right now. His hair is mussed. His eyes are warm. My warrior has taken off his armor for the night.

"Sadie and Penny seem cute," I venture. Scrub, scrub. Lather, lather. "What do you think?"

"It won't last."

"Someone's cynical tonight."

"It's true. Sadie will eat her alive."

"I thought that was a *good* thing in lesbian culture."

"Speaking of eating." He's behind me now—I can feel the warmth of his body. He puts down his glass and latches his strong fingers in the waistband of my pants. "You're a snack," he murmurs in my ear.

I chuckle. "You've been drinking."

"And I just downed a glass of water."

"I don't think it works *quite* that fast." His lips tease my throat. The sharpness of his teeth makes me gasp. "You should go to bed."

"Only if you come with me."

"I will. In just a minute."

"Can't wait a minute."

Eric North is used to getting what he wants. And why wouldn't he be—he's rich, famous, and his body is so attractive, he's contractually obligated (I'm not kidding about this) to have *at least* one shirtless scene in every one of his movies.

He turns me around to face him. The counter bites into my rear as he presses me into it, and he kisses the corner of my mouth. My hands are wet, but I loop my fingers into his jeans, holding him in place. I like his weight on me.

"You're aggressive tonight," I notice.

"You like it."

He's not wrong about that. I get weak in the knees when he gives me *that look*—when his blue eyes go sharp and hard. *Dominant* doesn't even begin to describe Eric North.

But this is different. When he kisses me fully on the lips, I taste how frantic he is. He's desperate. Manic. Wound tight by all the pressure of *everything* that's on his shoulders.

And he wants to fuck it all away. Well, I'm happy to distract, but if my body is going to be used, it'll be on my terms.

"Open your mouth," he says, so I do. He cups my face in his hand and presses his thumb past my teeth. His hands are huge, and I feel the digit explore my teeth, grip my jaw. I wrap my lips around it and swirl my tongue around his thumb suggestively.

The act draws a growl from him—a sound that always makes my toes curl. "Be a good boy and get on your knees," he demands.

I put my hand on his wrist and remove it from my face. "No," I tell him simply.

His eyes flicker with confusion at the foreign word. "No?"

"No," I repeat firmly. Then I draw my fingers through his hair—through the salt-and-pepper, down to the greying bits on the edge. "Be a good boy and get on *your* knees."

I rarely take control. Those aren't the roles that we're familiar with. I expect a protest from him, maybe. Instead, the look in his eyes shifts. I deepen the pressure on his head, and he lets me, lowering himself to the floor.

Ninety-nine percent of the time, Eric is a gargoyle—stone-cold and assertive. But every now and then, in the safe quiet of our relationship, he's a complete puppy dog. Just for me. He needs this as much as I do—I can tell by the way he grips my hips and nuzzles my crotch. The friction draws a lengthy sigh from me. His large fingers fumble open my pants, and he pulls my cock out, already half-hard for him and growing in his hand. Those eyes—grey blue and stormy—meet mine as he takes me in his mouth.

My breath goes ragged as my cock swells to full mast between his lips. It's the look in his eyes that gets me, that hungry, ravenous look—he's the wolf that could devour little Red in one bite but nibbles her toes instead.

"Good boy," I murmur, knowing that this feral man is domesticated only for me. I rake my fingers through his hair, nails on his scalp, and the noise that leaves him is somewhere between a growl and a purr. He swallows me into the velvet warmth of his mouth, and my head falls back as I moan.

God bless Eric North. I'm well-endowed, and yet he takes me without complaint, swallowing me to my hilt.

It's good, it's *very good*, and my self-control breaks. I've forgotten about the dishes, the party, the cleanup, the closet, Eric's twisted manager, and the deal they made with Chrys—nothing matters except me, him, and the pleasure that twists deliciously through my entire body with every contraction of his throat and swipe of his tongue.

"Fuck," I swear, words tumbling from my lips, "God, you're so good...I love you...I love you, I love you, *te amo...*"

His head bobs underneath my fingers; he reads my body impeccably, knows exactly where to lick and suck to draw me to my precipice. I'm there, hanging on the edge when he pulls back. When I leave his lips, I'm throbbing and coated in his saliva, and the air feels too cold.

He rises to his feet—and he's my Eric again, and I'm his—and when he pulls me into a crushing kiss, I know I'll do whatever he wants.

"Take off your clothes," he demands, his voice low and hoarse.

I do, quickly unbuttoning my shirt and pushing my pants the rest of the way off my legs. He yanks his shirt over his head and leaves his jeans in a heap on the floor with mine.

And—God. He's a sight. Broad chest, smattered with dark curly hair that drops like sand from an hourglass down his middle. Those tight abs, bulging biceps. His cock is stiff, meaty, and the sight of it makes my own mouth water.

He guides me onto the kitchen island—the very island

16

that, not hours ago, I was slicing bell peppers on for dinner—and hoists me on top of it. We kiss as he positions me how he wants me, on the edge of the table, underneath him, my legs hooked around his hips.

He stalls, though, and I notice him glancing around the kitchen.

"What are you—?"

My question is answered when Eric grabs the bottle of olive oil, shakes it out into his palm, then sets the bottle back down and lubricates his shaft with oil.

I laugh. "What am I now, a salad?"

"Call me Caesar," he murmurs as he hovers over me, one hand planted beside my head, the other positioning himself at my entrance.

"Hail—" I start, but that's the only word I get out before my breath leaves my body in a sharp gasp.

Eric is big, and no matter how many times we have sex (which is a lot), he always makes me see stars with the first thrust. I grip his arm tightly, and my legs fall to the side, forcing myself to relax into it. The muscles of his bicep flex against my hand as he rolls against me, moving in and out of me. He kisses my throat, nibbles my collarbone, my chest. The first jolt of pain quickly dissolves into pleasure, and I begin to moan.

He picks up the pace, thrusting over me, diving in deeper. Just when I think nothing can feel better, he wraps his oil-slick fingers around my dick and begins pumping me. My thighs tremble, hooked onto his hips, and there's nothing I can do now to stop the pleasure bursting from me.

Eric kisses me right as I cry out. My whimpers are lost inside his mouth as he strokes my orgasm from me; I coat my chest, my stomach. I'm a mess, panting and licking the inside of his mouth as he gives a final shuddering thrust, a deep groan, and spills over inside of me.

Pleasure ebbs and flows between us, and we lie here for a

moment, catching our breath. I love him like this, blissed-out, his heavy weight on top of me, all of his worries—for a moment—gone.

My thigh is starting to cramp around his waist, but I don't want to move, not yet. I hold him against my chest, my fingers deep in his hair, and he scoops me into his arms, his hand on the back of my neck.

We're tangled, sweaty, spent. But we can't stay here forever.

"I love you," he murmurs. When he says it like this—his voice heavy and thick—I know he means it.

I twist his hair between my fingers. "I love you too."

"I don't want to go."

"*Je sais, mon amour,*" I urge into his ear. "But it's *France.*"

5

ERIC

I feel like I got hit by a fucking steamroller.

My skull is throbbing, the back of my throat is thick, and the sunshine is piercingly loud.

It's 6:00 a.m. when my driver collects me and my baggage and takes us to a private hangar thirty minutes away. I don a pair of sunglasses and a baseball cap, but I know I'm not fooling anyone.

She's here. The girl. Chrys.

The plan is to fly in together. Download on the flight over. And I'm very aware I'm making a piss-poor first impression.

But I very much don't want to be here. I don't want to be drinking in recycled air for the next ten hours. I want to be back in our bed, with Nico's warm body slotted perfectly against mine.

My driver dumps me out in front of the private jet. I tip him, peel myself out of the car, and climb the ramp inside.

The Boeing 737 is spacious—complete with plush seats, a minibar, and a flat-screen TV. But I notice her immediately.

Chrys is as her headshot described her: five foot four, a hundred and thirty pounds, red hair, olive-green eyes. Cute-pretty, not bombshell pretty. Always a supporting actress, never a leading lady.

What they failed to mention is her smile. I can see why she and Nico are friends. It's what Nico calls an "Anansi" smile. Trouble. It says *I'm the girl who will get you stoned at the family dinner on Thanksgiving.*

"Well, it's about time," she tells me—what is that accent? Jersey? Nico set me up with *Jersey*? "We were about to fly by your house and scoop you up."

I fold into the seat beside her. I'm too broad, and my shoulders never fit the seats right. I extend a hand. "Eric."

"Chrys."

We shake hands. I underestimated how incredibly uncomfortable this would be.

"Thank you for doing this," I tell her.

She shrugs. "I owed Nico. Besides, I'm considering this an audition."

"Right. You're an actress."

Her eyes brighten at that. "Yeah, well, not quite on your level, but I've been in a handful of plays, a couple TV spots— you might've seen me in a tuna fish commercial. *We turn TuNa into TuYes!* It became a meme, sort of went viral."

She's peppy. Too peppy. My forehead throbs. "Must've missed that one."

She barrels forward. "So, should we get our story straight? Where we met, how long we've been together, how you proposed—?"

"Oh. Right." I shift in my seat, reach into my pocket, and pull out a small pull-string bag. I empty the contents into my palm—two engagement rings. I hold hers out for her. "Your costume piece."

"Thanks." She slips it on. It's a round gem. Bright. Deep red. It fits perfectly on her hand.

"Ruby." She blinks. "My birthstone. How—?"

"Nico picked it out."

20

A small smile from her. "I love it."

I ease mine over my finger. It's a simple band, but it feels noose-tight.

This knot in my throat won't relax.

For a moment, neither of us says anything.

"I was thinking," she pipes up again, "maybe you brought me to dinner? I know it's cheesy, but I'm such a sucker for the whole ring-in-the-dessert thing—"

"I'm hungover," I state abruptly. "I haven't slept all night. I'm not really into talking right now."

"That's fine. I brought this whole book of crossword puzzles." She waves to the small book in her lap. "I know you can do it on your phone, but I'm an old-fashioned pencil-and-paper kind of girl. It's just way more satisfying when you can't ask the computer for a hint—"

"Maker's Mark," I tell the approaching flight attendant, "on the rocks, please."

When she returns with my drink, I use it to knock back an Ambien. And I sink into my seat like a sedated horse.

"Alright, crossword," I hear Chrys murmur to her book as I put on my sleep mask, "time to meet your maker."

* * *

It's late when we land in Paris.

We don't see the Eiffel Tower, the Louvre, or the Notre-Dame.

I see, in order, the hangar bay, the parking lot behind the hotel, the lobby, the room key, the king-sized bed, and then the backs of my eyelids.

In the morning, I forget where I am, and I reach for Nico. My hand comes back with nothing but starched sheets.

Chrys and I share a suite. Two bedrooms. I don't have to see her until I'm ready to see her, and I'm not ready. It takes

21

me two hours to shower, shave, and finally start to feel a little more like myself again.

I'm scheduled for a panel at CrimeCon, a convention for mystery, thriller, and horror film fanatics in a little over an hour. My prep for public speaking events is a lot like my trailer time before shooting a scene. I have to take a minute and embody the character they want to see.

Eric North. Action star. Heterosexual. Loves beaches and red wine. Hates cats.

My backstory? I've spent my years as a bachelor on the prowl, until I met my one true love, Chrys.

My motivation? Get them to buy the ruse…and the movie ticket.

When I'm ready, I exit my room, feeling like I sprayed on too much cologne, wondering if I can dab some of it off before the panel.

I don't know what I was expecting to see, but it wasn't this… Chrys, in a robe, her hair twisted up in a towel like soft serve. She clasps her hands together as she sees me and exclaims, "You're up!"

"I'm up," I confirm.

"Great! Where to first? Should we have croissants and coffee in a chic café? Stroll down the cobblestone streets? Oh! Can we see the Eiffel Tower?"

Her excitement is at an eleven. I haven't had enough coffee for this.

"First time in France?" I ask.

"Is it obvious?"

I slip my Rolex around my wrist and strap it on with one hand. "I have to be at the convention from noon to six."

"I'll come with you."

I shake my head. "Stay here. Order room service."

Her mouth corkscrews. "Okay, not to sound ungrateful… but you did fly me halfway across the world to be your arm candy. And now you're relegating me to the hotel?"

"Listen, Candy—"

"Chrys."

"Chrys," I repeat. "I'll let you know when I need you."

I'm not trying to be an asshole. But Chrys is here to provide a service—nothing more, nothing less.

Which means no sightseeing, no baguettes, no fun. This is a business trip and should be conducted as such.

Even if my "business" is a peppy, redheaded cheerleader.

I try to soften the blow with "There's a spa. A pool. Get whatever you want."

Watch on, blazer on, I check my pockets once and then go to leave.

As the door closes behind me, I hear, "At least leave me a room key!"

I crouch and pass the room key under the door.

6

NICO

*M*y phone clatters on my nightstand.

I reach out to grab it. Normally, my arm would collide with Eric's warm body on the way to my phone. Instead, it slices through thin air. I pick up the phone and peel back my sleep mask. The lighted words on the phone vibrate as my eyes adjust in the dark.

It's one in the morning, and Chrys' number pops up on my phone.

A shiver of fear goes through me. Why would she be calling?

I put the phone to my ear. "Hello?"

"I spy with my little eye...something that starts with the letter *V*."

A momentary pause to go through my mental Rolodex. "Vodka?"

She gasps. "Oh, you're *good* at this."

"Are you drunk?"

"No, but I might be later."

I let out a deep sigh. "Okay," I tell her, "talk to me."

* * *

And she does. We talk. For hours.

Me: "What's your sign?"

Her: "Cancer."

Me: "Ah, Cancer. The emotional one."

Her: "It's true. I cry at sad commercials."

Me: "That sounds right. I'm a Virgo. He's an Aries."

Her: [gasping] "The ram. That explains *everything*."

* * *

Me: "Antonio Banderas, Monica Bellucci, and Brad Pitt."

Her: "Fuck Antonio, marry Monica, and kill Brad Pitt."

Me: "Not a fan of *Fight Club?*"

Her: "Overrated, but mostly, I am *still* not over Jennifer Aniston."

Me: "Ah, love is tragedy."

* * *

Her: "How long have we been on the phone?"

Me: "Two hours."

Her: "What do you think the roaming charge is on that?"

Me: "The production company is paying for your phones, aren't they? Scalp the bastards."

* * *

Me: "He's really not that bad, you know."

Her: "Maybe to you, but I'm pretty sure he hates me."

Me: "Eric can be slow to warm."

Her: "Any helpful tips?"

Me: "He's a brute on the outside, but a puppy dog underneath."

Her: "So I should start chucking tennis balls?"

Me: [Laughing, then quiet] "When you kiss him…run your fingers through his hair. He likes that."

* * *

I'm lying on my bed, watching the ceiling. We've lapsed into one of those comfortable silences, the ones where someone is going to say soon, *Well, I should let you go.*

But I don't want this conversation to end. And neither does she. I can feel she needs the companionship, maybe more than I do.

Why did we ever let so much time and space come between us?

"How did you meet Eric?" she asks.

"Have you seen the movie *Second Hand Kill?*"

"I missed that one, sorry."

"You and most of America. That movie was based off of my book, *Three O'Clock Shadow.*"

She gasps, "I *loved* that one."

"Thank you. They took some liberties with the movie, mind you—added some sex and car chases to make my modern noir palatable for the mainstream audience."

"Wasn't Eric in that movie?"

"He was. He played my dashing hero, Isaac Black. The production company paid me handsomely for the rights to my work, and I never heard from them again. Truthfully, I'm not even sure the scriptwriter read the source material.

"Eric did. Which, honestly, surprised me. Considering his past performances, I assumed the extent of his character work was hitting the gym. I was wrong. He read my book and called me almost every day. And this was before filming! He wanted to know Isaac's backstory—what his parents were like, how he'd grown up. He wanted to know my thoughts on the character's motivations, why he acted a certain way, did he *truly* love Lola or was she just a passing fancy…?

"It started on the phone, but eventually, we were meeting regularly. I'd have him over once or twice a week. We'd eat lunch on the back patio and discuss the character.

"I was...in a bad place at the time. For some writers, getting their work auctioned off would be a dream come true. For me, this was the end of my dream. I had just about given up on writing. I didn't sell the rights because I wanted to see what would become of it—I wanted to be *done* with it. This novel that I had spent *years* working on was about to become a summer box-office flop, stripped of all meaning and stuffed with cheap one-liners and 3-D special effects.

"I felt like a failure. I couldn't write. I couldn't sleep. I'd started drinking rather heavily. I was depressed but functional; no one around me, not even my mother, had a clue how bad it'd gotten. I daydreamed about downing a bottle of sleeping pills and tossing myself in the pool. It was *that* bad."

Chrys sighs. "Oh, Nico. I had no idea."

"No one did. At least, that's what I thought. My meetings with Eric—they'd become the highlight of my week. His questions started shifting, less about the characters, more about myself. He'd become my therapy session. And he was a great listener—he would sit there and say nothing, let me ramble and vent. Then finally, one night, when I'd spent all day talking and he'd spent all day listening, he turned to me and said, '*No one knows how much pain you're really in, do they?*'

"It stuck with me. No one *did* know, because I'd let my pride get in the way of asking for help. Eric, quite literally, saved my life. I asked for help. Stopped drinking. Started seeing a *real* therapist. Started writing again—I've published two novels since."

"That's great, Nico. I'm proud of you."

"Thank you."

"So when did it get...romantic?"

"Well...let's just say it got *physical* before it became romantic. We held off on committing as long as we could...

27

he didn't want to draw me into his world, I worried that my emotional baggage would be too much for him to carry. But we were compatible. In every aspect. We fell in love. You can't always help that."

"Do you wish you could?"

"No. Not for a second."

"It sounds like you two are happy together."

I swallow my tongue. The silence around me feels heavy. The air compresses. To her credit, she lets me have my silence. She lets me work through my ivy-tangle of thoughts.

"I think that's what worries me, truthfully," I confess after a while.

"What does?"

"That no one knows."

"Knows what?"

"How much pain he's in."

7

ERIC

*T*he flash of cameras nearly blinds me.

I smile through it. Always smile. As the crowd claps, roars, and whistles in a haze of black smudges behind the overhead lights.

Being at the convention gives me a strange two-way mirror illusion. I can see the people on stage beside me—Raul at the speakers' table to my right and our host, Grant Lizzy, to my left. Microphones and mini bottles of water on the table in front of us. But beyond the stage? The crowd is a fuzzy cloud of smoke, a sea of noise and excitement.

I can practically taste their sweat; it's that dank in this room.

Grant sits in his chair, notepad of questions in front of him, and smiles. I like Grant—he's a weird kid. Messy bleached hair, gauges in his ear, and ripped jeans, but he's wearing a blazer to class up his couch-potato outfit. Good attitude on him, though, and he's been doing his best to make all of us feel at ease on stage.

I need it. I'm not at ease. Put a camera in front of me. Give me lines. Give me a character. *That* I can do. But put me in front of a crowd of people and ask me just to *be myself?*

I haven't stopped sweating since I sat down. I'm glad I'm wearing my blazer. Hides the stains.

"So, Eric," Grant starts, with that unwavering smile, "our big action movie star!"

A ripple of laughter through the crowd. I smile so hard my molars hurt.

"This film is a bit of a departure for you, *non*? What made you take the role?"

I clear my throat and lean forward to speak into the microphone. "No one made me take it. I read it. Fell in love with the role. I saw an opportunity. To be more than..." I lean into my elbows, rub my hand up my arm self-consciously. "...a guy who blows things up."

"We're certainly itching to see this new side of you," Grant says.

"So am I," I reply.

"I love you, Eric North!" A woman's voice screams shrilly from the black cloud.

I chuckle and wink at the mass. "Love you more."

A chorus of hollers and shouts. My stomach churns under the attention.

"And Raul," Grant continues, and my gut unpinches once the eyes move away from me and onto the fidgety Cuban at my side, "they're calling this your big breakout role. Do you agree?"

Raul launches forward toward the microphone, nearly toppling his bottle of water. "Oh, yes, thank you. That is kind of you to say. Yes! I certainly hope so. I am among giants here, no?"

"What was it like to work with Eric North?"

"Oh—he is easy, so easy to work with. Very professional. And so handsome! I mean, look at this man." He slings an arm around my shoulder, and I tense. "It is not hard to love acting with him, no?"

He's leaning on me now—I feel the weight of his body on my shoulders—and the crowd eats it up, cheering him on. Even Grant laughs. "It seems like you two really get along."

Then Raul looks at me, his mouth crooked in a leering smile. "I could tell you…but I think it would be best to show you, no?"

My heart drops into the floor. The crowd loses it—cheering, shouting at us to kiss. I feel the beat against my rib cage, and I can feel Raul's body weight shifting closer.

Before he can lean in for a kiss, I grab the microphone and get out, "You'll have to pay the ticket fee to see that."

Disappointed groans from the audience. Grant swiftly recovers and moves the interview along. But I can barely hear it for the blood pounding in my ears. The rest of it is a blur, and eventually, it ends to the tune of fans cheering and chanting for us.

We cross the stage and take the steps backstage. Once we're in the wings, the techies start to pull the microphones from our shirts. As soon as both Raul's and my wires have been removed, I descend. I grab him by the front of his shirt as the techies scatter and slam him up against the wall.

"You touch me like that again," I growl, "and I'll tear your arm off. Is that understood?"

Raul gapes—this dumb, openmouthed expression—and I want to slap it off his face. I leave him like that—slack-jacked fucking idiot—and barrel past a couple of stunned volunteers.

"Hey—Eric!" Raul shouts when he finally gets his voice back. "It's a joke! Just a joke! We're still compadres, no?"

No.

It's not a joke to me.

It's my fucking life. And his little gay-for-the-camera stunt makes me feel unclean. Covered in stares. Toenail clippings in my teeth kind of bad.

I was *going* to stay, take a couple of pictures with con kids, but that plan is null and void now because I can't stop shaking. My vision blurs, and my heart won't stop pounding. I've got that light-headed feeling that always signals an oncoming panic attack.

Not here. Not now.

I cross backstage and throw myself into the nearest bathroom, locking the door. Part of me wants to lie down on the cool tiled floor, but the sensible, rational part of me knows it's a disease-ridden cesspit down there, so I turn on the sink instead, flip the water to cold, and start splashing my face with it.

I want to call my publicist. Or Nico. Someone. Anyone.

No.

I want to call my mom. I want to call my mom and tell her the kids in the playground are teasing me again and can she come pick me up?

But I haven't made a call like that since I was six. After my parents got divorced, I tried it, once, with my father. He scoffed and told me to stop being such a fag and suck it up.

I turn my gaze to the mirror and try to control my breathing. I look a lot like him, now. My father. Our hair greys the same—from the sideburns up. Same steel-blue eyes. He was built like a house too. Scary guy when you're six and your knees are bleeding.

I let the cool water drip down my neck, seep into my shirt. I stare at the guy in the mirror.

"Suck it up," he tells me. "Fucking pull it together."

I solidify. I stop trembling. I yank a paper towel free and dry off my face before tossing it in the bin. Unlatch the door and exit.

There's a bustle of people outside, so I grab the nearest woman with the "Staff" tag attached to her con lanyard hanging around her neck. "Hey. I've gotta sign some autographs. Where should I be?"

Her eyes widen—she must've seen my outburst with Raul
—but she composes well with a smile. "This way." I follow
the click of her heels. After a second, she glances over her
shoulder at me. "Are you okay?"

"I'm fine," I lie. And then we enter the fray, and cameras
swallow me again.

* * *

It's late by the time I get back to the hotel. Almost nine.

But my blood still feels like it's on fire. I sign some autographs in the lobby and then take the elevator upstairs.

My key card doesn't take the first three times, and I swear
at it, smack it, and finally the light turns green and the door
unlocks. When I get inside, the air feels ten degrees colder.
Chrys seems oblivious to it. She's in a small dress with her
foot on the table. She's painting her toes seashell pink.

"How was the con?" she asks.

"Fine." I rip off my blazer and fling it over the back of the
chair.

Her eyes flick over me. A slender eyebrow rises. "Are you
okay?"

I wish people would stop asking me that.

"I'm fine."

Her feet are on the table, the dirty room service cart in
the middle of the room. I'm as raw as a cracked oyster.
Everything has me on edge.

She wiggles her toes. "Can you say any words other than
fine?"

"Yes. Get dressed," I tell her, my voice coming out a bit
rougher than I intend it. "We're going out tonight."

Her eyes light up. "*Out*?" she repeats. "Like *out*, out?
Thank God—I'm dying of cabin fever. What should I wear?"

"Clothes. Nice clothes."

I go into my bedroom, close the door, and lock it. I need

at least thirty minutes of warm-up. Shower. Change. Scrub my face.

Then it's showtime. The cameras. Chrys.

One big fucking show.

8

ERIC

*W*e end up at a top-scale restaurant in the city center. While they prepare our table, Chrys and I head to the bar to have a drink.

I take the corner at the far end, near the kitchen. "I'll have a—"

"Maker's Mark. On the rocks. And I'll have a Shirley Temple, please."

I lift my eyebrows at Chrys. "How…?"

"You ordered it on the plane." She taps the side of her head. "Memory of an elephant. I was a continuity supervisor for a while when I was trying to get my foot in the door."

"And now you're the tuna girl."

The bartender returns with our drinks. She wraps both of her hands around her glass.

"It's a hard life, but someone's gotta do it." She smiles around her straw. "We don't have to talk about me."

"What do you want to talk about?"

"I spoke to Nico."

Cue my heart, kicking like a caged rabbit inside my chest. "Okay."

"He's doing fine, thanks for asking. He misses you."

"I'm not doing this with you."

"Doing *what?*" She lifts a hand. "Besides Nico, I'm the only person who *knows*. You have to talk to someone. Bottling things up is no good for anyone. Least of all you. My uncle bottled up his emotions, and now he has diabetes. True story."

I stare at her a moment. "I'm going to make a couple assumptions about you," I say.

She shrugs. "Assume away."

"You're great at auditions. You always get called back. But you never get picked for the headliner. Always the supportive friend. The caring mom. The hypochondriac sister."

"Maybe, so what? It's not a big deal—"

"Yes. Yes, it is a big deal. In Hollywood, your career is only half talent. The other half is presence."

"I get that you work in front of the flashy cameras with million-dollar budgets...and I appreciate your advice. I really do. But when someone hires me, I don't want it to be because I tricked them into it. I want the response to be more..."

"What?"

"Genuine."

"What are you saying? That I'm all show?"

"No. That's what you're saying. That's what you *just* said." She eats the cherry off her stem, then points the stem at me. "My turn. I'm going to make a couple assumptions about *you.*"

I fold my arms over my chest and brace.

"You've never lost. Ever. To anyone. You think that makes you invincible, but it doesn't. You don't let anyone climb your tall walls, because if they do, they'll see that you're nothing more than a paper man."

"A *paper man?*"

"Yep. Looks all big and tough, but one blow and you

knock him over." She cocks her head, poodle-like. "How am I doing?"

The waiter comes by, and I tell him, "We'll take the check."

She blinks. "But we haven't had dinner—"

"Get it to go," I tell her in a tone that leaves no room for argument.

* * *

We leave carrying doggy bags.

I'm in a rotten mood, I feel like a rotten person, and I just want to go to my hotel room and vanish.

But as soon as we exit, there are cameras waiting for us.

"Miss Hudson!" one of the cameramen exclaims, snapping his camera like she's a dancing monkey, "Give us a smile, yes?"

She puts a hand on her hip, juts to the side, and poses. I have to hand it to her. The camera does love her.

"Yes!" the cameraman shouts. "Now, Mr. North! Come! You are in love, yes? It is the city of love! How beautiful!"

Chrys tilts her chin toward me, questioning. I know what her eyes are asking.

This is why I hired her, isn't it?

I've kissed women before. Actresses I've worked alongside. Sorority girls I'd tried to impress in my frat boy days. That one woman at a tiki bar in Miami a couple of years ago, after a big fight with Nico, when I was drunk and frayed and hating myself.

It's felt wrong every time. A deep, inexplicable wrong. A lie with lips, and teeth, and tongues.

So when she looks at me now, I know what's coming, and I feel it—that knife twist in my gut.

But I play the game. It's acting. It's only acting.

I tilt in to meet her lips and kiss her for the camera. I rest my hand on her waist in a way that I know will play well for the audience.

This is a role, and if I'm nothing else, I'm a fucking good actor.

But then she does something that throws me. As our mouths meet, her nails comb through my hair, running up my scalp and down the back of my neck.

And that gesture takes the breath out of me, because in that moment, I see—

Nico.

9

ERIC

$\mathscr{I}$t's five years ago.

I'm in Nico's living room, my wet clothes dripping obscenely onto his very nice oriental rug. He sits on his leather chaise, towel around his shoulders, staring off into nothing.

"What the hell were you thinking?" I growl.

"I wasn't."

"That's for damn sure." I'm pacing, my earlier panic flaring into anger now.

"It's fine." Nico's voice is hollow. His eyes are red-rimmed. "I'm fine."

It's a punch in the gut. Because *I'm fine* are not the words someone should use after they just nearly drowned at the bottom of their own pool.

I crouch down in front of him, my hands on his knees. I *need* him to look at me. "You're not fine," I tell him, and his eyes grow wet. "If I hadn't been here—"

"You were here," he interrupts. Then he lets out a noise— a frustrated, strangled half sob. "*Why* were you here? Of all nights, Eric…"

He's right. I wasn't supposed to come tonight.

Which hurts. He'd *counted* on being alone. He'd counted on no one being here to pull him out of the pool and save him.

"You're soaking wet. Let's get you out of these."

I pull his shirt from his head and let it flop to the ground. He lets me, placidly lifting his hands like a doll. I take the towel and dab it over his neck, through his hair.

I'm putting back together the pieces of the man who's fallen apart in front of me.

"Please," he says suddenly, and his voice is so soft, it startles me. "I need to know. Why did you come here tonight?"

His eyes shimmer. He looks so earnest, and I know I can't lie to him. Not now.

So I make my confession:

"I came here to do this."

Then I kiss him, softly, on the lips.

My heart is pounding. My chest is tight.

But then Nico kisses me back. He flattens himself against the chaise and parts his legs, his body consenting. Inviting me closer.

I kiss him. And I kiss him. And I kiss him.

His fingers rake through my hair, all the way to my scalp, and when he grips, he clings so hard, it hurts—

10

ERIC

I grab her wrist, hard. Too hard.

Chrys stops and blinks at me, emerald eyes startled.

"What are you doing?" I hiss at her. My heart won't stop pounding—that ugly, thick beat.

"Eric." She intones my name softly, as a warning. It means *people are watching.* It means *retract your claws.*

I force myself to soften. I release her wrist, and we break apart. The paparazzi are harassing us, begging to have another kiss, but I hail a cab and usher her inside before I can do any more damage tonight.

We return to the hotel room. I drop my doggy bag in the minifridge.

"What's next on the agenda?" Chrys asks, kicking off her heels. "Pay-per-view? A rousing game of Parcheesi?"

I end the conversation by closing my bedroom door.

11

NICO

"*I* know I need to tell her. I just like the way this feels, you know?"

I sit across from Alex and stab at my lettuce. We're enjoying a light lunch on the restaurant patio as he regales me with his latest romantic drama.

There is *always* drama. We are the queers of LA, after all.

"What do you think?" he asks me. His bottom lip pouts with concern, lip ring protruding.

"I..."

My phone buzzes on the white linen tablecloth. The text pops up:

[text: Chrys] How do you put up with him?

I clear my throat and click to darken the screen, trying to refocus my attention on my friend. "Everything at its own time," I tell him. "If she cares about you, she'll understand."

"I know," he sighs. "Things are just going good now. Really good. I don't want to rock the boat."

Another distracting buzz from my phone. And another.

[text: Eric] I can't do this.
    [text: Eric] She's fucking impossible.
    [text: Eric] This whole thing is a fucking mess.

Across from me, Alex's eyebrows lift. "You're popular this morning. Do you need to answer that?"

I press my mouth into an apologetic smile. "I'm so sorry. Trouble in paradise. One moment."

Alex lifts his palm. "Do what you have to."

I don't text over meals—I can't think of anything ruder. So I make this quick. I start a group thread between the two of them and me.

[Group Text: Nico, Eric & Chrys]
    [text: Nico] Eric, meet Chrys.
    [text: Nico] Chrys, Eric.
    [text: Nico] You are both in the same time zone. I am not. Goodnight.

Then I silence my texts, put my phone in my pocket, and turn my attention back to my friend.

"I'm sorry," I tell him. "I'm all ears."

ERIC

*T*hat bastard.

I sit on the edge of my plush, crimson-red bedspread and stare at Nico's group message.

I've been a pinball bouncing between anxiety and rage all fucking day.

And *this* is what I get?

Can't talk now, deal with it your-fucking-self?

I grip the phone in my hand and nearly crack the case.

Control yourself, Eric.

I close my eyes.

If I were home, I could grab Nico by the hair, throw him over the couch, and fuck his brains out. I could release my anxiety with one huge, toe-curling orgasm.

Nico is, and will always be, my favorite coping mechanism.

But Nico isn't here now.

I glance at my bedroom door. It wears a cream paint job and an ornate, leaf-print handle.

Well.

Fuck it.

I stand. I go and open the bedroom door.

Across the neutral ground of the living space is Chrys'
bedroom. Her door, too, is open. She stands in the doorway.
She's dressed down for bed, in nothing but a long T-shirt
with some rock band on the front that hangs down to her
mid-thighs. Her red hair looks silken, recently brushed, and
falls down her shoulders in waves.

I, too, am in my comfortable clothes. Sweatpants and a
loose shirt.

No cameras. No paparazzi. No fans. We're just two
people now.

For a minute, we stand like this, mirror images of each
other. We say nothing. Her green eyes watch me, curious but
cautious. Like a small fox sizing up the farmer's intentions.

Finally, I break the silence. "Do you know how to play
chess?"

13

CHRYS

I didn't. But I do now.

Eric walks me through the chess basics. The setup, the strategy, and the rules.

The chess table is positioned next to a thin, floor-to-ceiling window that opens up to a narrow balcony. The night sky is inky black, twinkled with dotted lights. I can see the Eiffel Tower in the distance. It has a Christmastime vibe that makes me feel like a little kid.

"The idea," Eric says as he nudges his piece forward, "is to always be a step ahead of your opponent."

"You're used to that, aren't you? Always being a step ahead."

"I have to be."

"It must be exhausting."

He looks up from the chess game. That stormy, blue-eyed warning. *Don't come too close. I bite.*

"Your turn," he says.

Okay. One of us has to fall on their sword, and it's clearly not going to be him. I try: "Look. I'm sorry about what I said over dinner. It's not my place to tell you how to live your life.

You tell people what they want to hear, and that's fine. That's your choice."

"Haven't you ever told a lie?"

I shrug. "Hasn't everyone?"

"My point exactly."

"Right, but there's a tiny difference."

"What?"

"What you see is what you get with me."

"About…seeing you." His eyes scan me once. "Don't you have any pants?"

I arch my eyebrows. "Aren't you gay?"

"I'm still a man."

"Sorry, am I *distracting*?" I cross one leg over the other, and the hem of my shirt rides up my bare thigh.

Am I being a brat? Yes. But he's being a grumpus, and two can play at that game.

He averts his eyes from my legs and onto the chessboard. "Thin ice, kid," he growls and moves his piece.

"Just playing by your rules, Daddy-o." Gay or not, he must be *slightly* distracted, because he's left his queen defenseless. I lift my knight and claim his pawn, placing it in front of his queen. "Checkmate. I think I like this game."

"Beginner's luck," he says, and we reset.

14

NICO

J've returned home from lunch, and I'm sitting at my desk, attempting to write, when I get another text.

This one is private, from Chrys. It simply says, *Hey, give me a call when you're free.*

I consider it. I should be writing, but truthfully, I've been blocked since Eric left.

I'm worried about him. I can't help but worry.

I give in and finally call Chrys back.

"Is everything okay?" I ask her.

"Yeah…you were right. We just needed to work it out."

"That's good to hear."

But then she goes quiet for a moment, like she's picking her next words carefully. "I've been thinking," she says, "about this…bizarre little game we're playing. Wouldn't it be nice to be one step ahead?"

"I'm not sure I follow."

"This is going to sound crazy," Chrys says.

"Well, you *are* crazy."

"But I had a thought…"

She tells me her plan. I listen, quietly. Meanwhile, my

heart begins to race in my chest at the mere *implication* of her words.

She continues. "Before you say no—"

"No," I interrupt her. And then: "Well, maybe. I just don't know. What would Eric say?"

"Eric would say no."

"Right. Which is why we shouldn't do it."

"But in his heart, he would say yes."

"I don't think that's how that works."

"*Or...*"

I sigh. "Yes. Or."

15

ERIC

*D*ay two of the con goes smoother than day one.

Mostly because I get to spend four hours in a booth, rather than onstage. I sign autographs, I shake hands with fans, and most importantly, I don't have to deal with Raul and his passive-aggressive flirtations, because what the *fuck*.

I don't know French aside from a couple of choice phrases, but the staff helps to translate for me so I don't accidentally tell someone I want to skin their cat.

I've left Chrys at the hotel. Again. This is difficult enough without her here, and I don't need to be constantly looking over my shoulder.

There's a line ten people deep to my booth. I've just finished another picture and another autograph, when a too-familiar face approaches.

My heart falls in my fucking lap.

Chrys is there. And she's not alone. Beside her, looking out of place, clutching his wrist, shifting awkwardly from one leg to another...

It's Nico.

"Hey, babe," Chrys purrs, putting both palms on the booth and leaning forward.

"Hi," I say. Tone crisp. Curt. "What are you doing?"

"Oh, you know. I got bored spending all day at the hotel, so I thought—why not come out and see how my fiancé is doing?"

I press my mouth into a smile. "That's sweet."

We're surrounded by fans. Cameras. My heart is pounding.

"Oh!" As if she just remembered, she grabs Nico and pulls him in beside her. "I almost forgot—this is my friend Nico. He and I went to college together. He's in town researching his next novel, isn't that right?"

She's not outing me. The knowledge is a strange, sick brand of relief.

But he's still there. The way he looks at me, it's like he expects me to slap him.

"Ah—yes. My novel. A mystery. In Paris." His voice chirps in a pitchy way I've never heard before. He's stumbling over his words. He's not accustomed to improvising.

He's so goddamn cute, my heart pinches in my chest. Somehow, I keep my expression neutral.

"Nico." I say his name as though it's the first time saying it —as though I haven't repeated it a thousand times before. "I remember. We worked together before. *Second Hand Kill.* Small world."

"Small world indeed."

"Nice to see you again."

Then I extend my hand. He hesitates before taking it.

"You as well."

His hand feels so soft, so familiar in mine. Like an anchor, grounding me.

"I'm a bit busy right now," I tell the two of them, "but let's catch up later."

"Perfect!" Chrys squeezes Nico's arm. "We'll do dinner. Catch you then, hon!"

"Mmhm."

She drags Nico away. I watch them leave. I watch *him* leave. Those slim hips. The oversized sweater. His curly hair that just *begs* to be gripped.

"Mr. North?"

"Huh?"

I readjust my attention to my fans as someone shoves a picture of myself in front of me, alongside a Sharpie.

NICO

"This was a terrible idea," I say, the words flying out of my mouth as soon as we are out of earshot. "Utterly humiliating. The worst. Did you see the way he looked at me? He looked panicked. I shouldn't have come. This was all a terrible idea—"

"Nico." She has to skip ahead to get in front of my quick steps and physically brings me to a stop, her hands on my shoulders, her eyes level with mine. "Did you hear what he said?"

"What?"

"He said *it's nice to meet you.* He's happy you're here."

My mouth is dry, my heart pounds in my chest, but I let myself hear her words. I adjust my glasses on my face to give my hands something to do and force myself to swallow. Take a breath. "He did say that."

"*Yes.* He did." Her hands roll over my shoulders, soothing.

"It's just...I don't want to force his hand...or something to jeopardize him."

"What are you doing? You're *existing.* There's nothing wrong with that."

"Sometimes I wonder," I mutter.

"Look—we're not lying about anything. We *legitimately* went to college together. You're *legitimately* my friend. It's not strange or suspicious that you're here with me. It's the perfect cover! No one will suspect anything." She bumps her shoulder against mine. "Plus, he's happy you're here. More importantly—*I'm* happy you're here. Aren't you happy you're here?"

I button my lip. "Truthfully? I'm not sure yet."

"Well then—" She hooks her arm in mine. "—let's walk around the Louvre until you are."

17

ERIC

J have a meeting with Monica at 2:45 p.m.

One of the staff members directs me to a staging room, where I have semi-privacy. They've got a care station set up here—bottles of water, Doritos, and Band-Aids. I steal a bottle of water, pull my iPad out of my satchel, and set it up on the table.

Monica calls for a video chat, and I pop my earbuds in. We make small talk initially—she wants me to tell her about Paris. About the con. But most importantly…

"How are things with Chrys?"

"We had a rocky start," I tell her. "But…we're getting there."

"How so?"

"Well…she invited Nico here."

"Nico!" Monica's voice pitches, and her screen vibrates briefly. "Eric—no. Not a good idea. If anyone sees the two of you two together—"

"Yes, I know. Fire and brimstone."

She goes off on me. Meanwhile, my phone buzzes with a text.

I flip open my phone in my lap and check it. Chrys has

55

sent me a photo of her and Nico at the Louvre. They're both pouting, imitating the portrait of some very somber-looking Renaissance man.

I can't help it. I crack a smile.

"Is this *funny* to you, Eric?" Monica seethes on the other end of the screen.

I turn my phone on its face and turn my attention back to her. "No. It's not. I'm capable of handling myself around him."

"I hope that's true, because this is fishy to me. Why would she bring him here? Have you checked your room to see if it's bugged?"

"She hasn't…bugged my room…"

Another text. I resist the urge.

"Are you *sure*?" Monica protests. "If a video of you and Nico gets out, well, you can kiss your career goodbye—"

My phone buzzes again, and this time, I can't stop myself. I glance at the screen.

It's a picture of Nico doing a *perfect* Mona Lisa impression in front of the woman herself.

I burst out laughing. I can't help it. The image of Nico having fun like that…it unlocks something inside of me.

Laughter that I didn't know I had pent up comes spilling out. I haven't laughed this hard in *years.* Maybe ever. Before I know it, tears are spilling down my face, and I'm apologizing to Monica—or at least trying to—through wheezed gasps of laughter.

"Maybe we should take a break," she mutters in my ear, which just brings on a new bout of side-splitting laughter.

18

NICO

*P*aris, je t'aime.

Chrys and I go to the Louvre. The Centre Pompidou. We have a liquid lunch of red wine and a packed charcuterie board.

I pride myself on being well researched. Worldly, in a bookish way. Every sentence in my novels has been painstakingly drafted and redrafted to be truly authentic to the time and location of the story itself.

But I haven't realized what a small box I've been living in until I taste French air.

The only thing that would make it better? If he was here with us.

We're sitting outside at a café, and I'm breaking apart another piece of brie even though I *know* I don't need it, when Chrys looks at her phone and gasps. "I've got a text!"

"From?"

"The big bad wolf himself."

"What does it say, Red?"

She sets the phone on the table and turns it toward me.

. . .

[Eric]: Let's go out tonight.

[Eric]: Bring your friend.

Immediately, I feel the blood rush to my cheeks.

"You're blushing!" Chrys laughs.

"I'm...not...it's the red wine..." I tug uncomfortably at my turtleneck.

She squints at me. "Wait...have you two *ever* been on a date?"

"Well...yes and no. I've been to his house. He's been to mine. But not an in-public date, no."

She squeals and grabs my arm, squeezing. "Well, let's make it one to *remember*." She takes out her wallet and waves it. "We're going shopping."

ERIC

I watch the perspiration drip down the side of my pint glass. I catch small beads of cold water under my fingertips and trace them into the wood of the bar.

If I keep my head down, I tend to get approached by fewer fans. Generally, people can tell when you want to be left alone.

They're late. By ten minutes.

Now eleven.

Out of the edge of my vision, I see two figures enter Le Meurice. A flurry of red hair stands out from the crowd. I don't look up, however, until I hear, "Looking lonely, Eric. Need some company?"

I turn, ready to quip back, when—

I see him.

Chrys looks good—she's draped in a green velvet dress that brings out the color of her eyes and dangling, gold earrings.

But *Nico*.

He's tucked into a checkered button-up and tie, layered underneath a knit sweater and an olive-green blazer. His pants are fitted, and they accent the length of his legs, the narrow shape of his hips. He's cleaned up, his dark beard tracing his sharp jawline. Those gentle brown eyes look up at me hopefully from behind his glasses.

He sucks all of the air out of my lungs. It takes everything in me not to touch the soft cotton of his blazer. Or tug on the short cut of his beard.

My pants are tight, and my heart is full of thorns.

"You look good," I tell them. "Both of you."

But Nico seems nervous, hands clasping politely in front of him. "Shall we take a seat?" he asks, glancing over his shoulder like he expects an assassin on his tail.

"Right this way," the waiter says, guiding us to our table.

NICO

I must be a complete fool.

When we sit down at the table, I can't stop my hands from trembling. I've hidden under layers like a turtle, but now they feel oppressive, and I'm sweating underneath.

I am a thorn at the dinner table. The way Eric is looking at me...he must hate me. I've come unannounced. I've gotten in the middle of his façade. I've muddled very clear lines he's drawn to keep our lives in order—and for what?

I can't stop scanning the restaurant. Underneath the beautiful chandeliers, near the bar, I'm certain I see men and women with cameras. Everyone on their phones, tilting them ever so slightly in our direction.

"We should trade seats." I still Chrys almost as soon as we sit down. I'm sitting too close to Eric—she needs to be here, beside him. The thought of being caught on camera with him... My anxiety spikes.

"Oh. Are you sure?"

"It's fine," Eric says, the low thunder beside me. "Stay where you are."

So I do.

The waiter asks for our drink orders, and Eric orders for

the table. I have no idea what he's ordered—I can't hear over the blood rushing in my ears. Once the waiter leaves and it's just the three of us, a heavy tension takes root. For a while, no one says anything.

"I saw your pictures," Eric speaks finally, lifting the eons of silence between us.

"Oh?" I pipe up, eager to latch onto anything at this point. "Did you like them?"

"Mmhm."

"We checked out the Louvre," Chrys prompts.

Immediately, words start falling from me, rapid-fire. "Did you know they have an original Degas? I've seen it maybe a million times before but to see it right there, in person. It was a religious experience—"

"You should wash your hands," Eric interrupts suddenly.

"Sorry?"

"Your *hands*," Eric presses. "You should wash them."

By which he means *conference in the bathroom. Now.*

"Y-yes." My eyes flick between Eric, then Chrys—which is silly, because she can't protect me here—then back to Eric again. I clear my throat, lift my napkin, and refold it onto the table. "Well. I'll be right back."

I rise and leave. Eric doesn't meet my gaze, but seconds later, I hear his chair move as well.

I'm mid-lather when the bathroom door opens and closes. I glance up and see him.

Eric has murder in his eyes.

"Are we alone?" he asks. His voice is steely and cold.

"I…believe so…"

It doesn't matter what I think. He does a quick check, pressing each stall open until he's convinced it's just us. I take my time washing the soap from my hands before I turn off the faucet. It gives me approximately three seconds to gather myself. Pull it together. Steel myself off for the storm that is Eric's temper.

"What the hell are you doing here?" His voice is a low rumble—the calm before lightning strikes.

I will not show him how desperate I am to please him right now. Eric is a shark. If he smells blood, he'll go for the throat.

Instead, I straighten up, wipe my hands on a towel, and explain. "Well, I *was* washing my hands—"

"Don't be cute," he interrupts. "I'm stuck with one brat. I don't need two."

I sigh. "I'm just here as a friend, Eric. I can leave tomorrow, if you'd like."

"You know what it does to me to have you here."

"Yes. I know. I'm a strain on your career—"

"That's not what I'm talking about."

His eyes don't leave mine. And then it hits me.

Hold on…

Am I misreading the fire in his gaze?

He closes the distance between us so quickly that it startles me, and I take a step backward in retreat. My back hits the wall, and he catches my jaw in hand. "How am I supposed to have you so close… without kissing the hell out of you?"

My breath leaves my body as his thumb traces my lower lip. "I…I'm not…"

He removes my glasses from my face. "Stop talking."

Not that I could talk if I wanted to—his lips close roughly over mine.

Desire unpins inside of me and comes tumbling out—inside his mouth, against his hard body. We're grabbling, our touches ravenous. I grip his jacket and sink my fingers into the tough leather. He tugs at my belt until it yields to him, and then I feel the pull as he untucks my shirt and slides his palm inside. I feel the strength of his large hand

63

flat against my belly, and then his fingers nestle my zipper down.

"Do you know what it does to me?" he asks, his voice low, raspy, "Knowing that you're here...in my city...breathing my air...when I want nothing more than to be buried inside you?"

I can't answer—I choke on a gasp as his hand dives inside my briefs and he takes me in his grip. I'm undone, and it takes nothing at all to get me swollen and needy under his expert touch...those hands that have spent years mapping me, learning me.

His touch is rough. Unrelenting. He strokes me rapidly, and my eyes flutter closed.

My head drops back against the tile, and I can't stifle the moan that leaves me. I am his. Completely. His lips work my throat, that sensitive spot right underneath my ear, licking, sucking.

Breathlessly, I remind him, "No marks. Please."

His response is a feral growl.

I'm swept away by his veracity, and before long, I feel the pressure in my loins start to build. I can't hold off—not the way he's ravishing me. A whimper leaves me, and I cling to him tightly, thrusting into his hand, rutting my way to my release—

I no longer care about the cameras. Or the people outside. Or France, or any of it. All I can think of is the fire in Eric's eyes and the devilish way he rolls his thumb over the tip of me, sending me careening toward the edge of sanity.

And then, all at once, he stills. I'm panting, and I can feel myself leaking, throbbing in his grip.

"On second thought..." he says, and the darkness in his voice makes me shiver. "If I have to be in agony...so do you."

Slowly, he releases me from his grip and withdraws. I hold back a whimper. I feel as though I've been marooned at sea and his hand is the lifeboat, drifting away.

He moves his hand to my face again, and this time, when he presses his thumb to my lip, I taste the salt of myself on him. "You've been very a naughty puppy," he informs me.

"Yes."

"You're a mess. Clean yourself up, then come join us at the table. What are you not going to do?"

My face burns. "Finish myself."

"Why is that?"

"Because I'm yours, and yours alone."

His mouth connects with mine, and my tongue meets his desperately.

I am a masochist. Eric knows this. He feeds the monster inside of me.

He puts his hand on my chest and finishes the kiss, rationing my affection. He puts some distance between us, and at once, the hardness in his sharp blue eyes softens. "I am glad you're here," he says, and the genuineness in his tone makes my heart pound. The backs of my eyes sting, but I'm going to hold myself together, because now is not the time or place.

"Me too," I say, because it's all I can say when I'm this breathless, my throat this tight, my chest and cock both aching.

He examines me, as though he's checking a teacup for cracks, and then he says, "Come out when you're ready."

When he leaves, I can finally catch my breath.

21

ERIC

$\mathcal{C}$hrys and I sit alone at the table for almost thirty seconds before Nico reemerges.

"Everyone's hands clean?" Chrys asks.

"You could say that," I deflect.

Nico looks like he's been swept up in a hurricane. That lost-puppy look in his eyes makes my pants unbearably tight.

"Good," Chrys says. "I got hungry and ordered for the table."

"What did you order?"

"Everything. Oh! I almost forgot." Then she reaches behind her head, fiddling with a clasp on her dress. I blink, and the strap of her dress falls, revealing a thin, lacy bra underneath.

Immediately, I draw up my menu, holding it in front of her chest. "What the *fuck*?" I snap.

She has the audacity to look at *me* as though I've lost my mind. Then, without hurry, she pulls the strap back up and fixes the clasp on her dress. "You two were in there for ten minutes," she says. "And you both come out bright-eyed and red-faced. Now, do you think the paparazzi at the bar are going to talk about *that* tomorrow, or are they going to focus on my nip slip?"

I have to hand it to her. She has a point.

"Oh," Nico says. He looks shell-shocked. "I'm sorry," Nico stumbles out. "We shouldn't have...ah..."

"Thank you," I say. I look her in the eyes when I say it.

I mean it. She's done nothing but look out for us—meanwhile, I've been an asshole.

I've been hard on her. And hard on him.

I'm a hard guy to deal with.

"No need to thank me," she says and waves the menu, "but you *can* help me split this bread pudding."

22

ERIC

$\mathcal{W}$e almost make it back to the hotel without incident.

There's a small swarm outside the hotel, waiting for us. People with cameras, notebooks, and pens. When we get close, Nico slows his steps, dropping behind us.

Oh. Right. I'm supposed to be engaged.

It feels wrong to do this in front of Nico. Chrys catches my eyes. Hers look questioning. She's waiting to follow my lead.

I approach the crowd, all smiles. I autograph a couple of notebooks. Shake hands. Stand with fans for a couple of pictures. Before we head inside, I put my hand on the small of Chrys' back. She turns to me, and I press a small, chaste kiss to her lips.

It'll have to be enough. We head inside, and I pound on the button for the elevator.

I don't exhale until we're inside the elevator and the doors close. I can't look at either of them. I can feel Chrys beside me, picking at her dress, fidgeting uncomfortably.

Then, out of nowhere, Nico begins to chuckle.

I turn around and narrow my eyes at him. "What's so funny?"

"It's just…" He waves his hand. "I thought you were better actors."

"What do you mean?"

"That kiss was *horrendous*," he says. "Utterly unbelievable. I've seen you kiss your grandmother with more gusto."

I scoff. Chrys glances at me and shrugs. "He's not wrong."

"What the hell do you want me to do?" I snap. "You're right there."

"That shouldn't matter," Nico protests. "Do you think I don't see the pictures? The Twitter posts?"

I can feel my anger tightening in my shoulders. I don't want to talk about this. I don't want to think about it. I don't know why he's pushing this, right here, right *now*.

He extends a hand to Chrys. "My dear," he says, "if you would allow it, perhaps I can demonstrate?"

A smile breaks across her mouth. She pushes her hair over her shoulders and gives him her hand. "Permission granted."

"Good." Nico's eyes flicker to mine to make sure I'm watching him—and damn him, there's something mischievous in those glittering green eyes. His hand cups her face, and he tilts in so he's only inches away from her. "The intimacy of the kiss," he muses, "is all about appreciating the person across from you. Giving them your full attention. Letting them know that, right now, your world revolves entirely around them."

He's staring into her eyes as he talks. She looks mesmerized—a cobra dancing to his tune. His thumb dances across her plump bottom lip. "Is this okay?"

"Yes," she says. She's breathless.

My heart hammers as I watch Nico close his mouth over hers. Nico is gentle, taking his time with her—their lips meet, and slowly, he takes it deeper. She sighs into his mouth, their eyes falling closed as they share this intimate moment.

What the fuck. Jealously jumps through my veins. "That's enough," I growl.

Immediately, Chrys snaps out of it. She pulls back and blinks. "I'm—I'm sorry," she gets out.

But before she can say anything else, I grab her by the back of the head and kiss her roughly. I didn't plan it. Didn't expect it. But I need her. I need her mouth, I need to hear her sigh, I need to feel the softness in her lips as she submits to me, opening to me. I lash my tongue across hers, keeping her body flush against mine, and claim her.

I don't know how long we're like that. But the doors *ding* open, and we break apart.

She looks flushed. Her eyes are hazy, and her lips are swollen.

Me? My pants are tight; my heart feels full of thorns.

I lost control.

I fucked up.

None of this makes sense. I watched them kiss, and I got possessive. Of *her.*

I want them. *Both* of them. Right here. Right now.

Until Nico clears his throat, snapping us out of it.

"That was better," he says, and then: "I believe this is our floor."

His voice is calm, cool, and unaffected. I don't know how he can be so calm about this.

Thank God the hallway is empty. We step down it, and I open the door with my key card. Once we're inside, Nico puts his hand on my arm.

"Eric," he says gently. "Can we talk?"

"About *what?*" I cross my arms over my chest.

"The kiss," Nico says plainly.

"You kissed her first," I counter.

"Yes. To make a point."

"What point?"

He wets his lips. He's choosing his words carefully. "You care about her."

"I don't know what you're talking about."

"Alright. I'll be clearer. You're attracted to her."

I scoff. "I haven't been with a woman since college."

"Sexuality is fluid," he says with the patience of a teacher. "People change."

"I don't."

"It's okay. I'm not mad."

"Then why are we talking about this?"

"Because I'd be open to it."

"Open to *what?*"

"A threesome." The proposal hangs in the air before he adds, "Oh, I suppose we are in France. A *ménage à trois*, if you will."

I growl, "You're out of your mind."

"Eric." He steps forward, and his palms rest on my chest. "Are you being resistant to this because you don't want it...or because you're afraid of wanting it *too* much? This isn't a trick. There isn't a right answer. I promise, I wouldn't have brought it up if I was uncomfortable with it."

"How do we know *she's* into it?"

"We'd ask her. Of course. But I'd wager a guess. Besides." He adjusts his glasses. "It wouldn't be the first time."

A volcano rises inside of me. I feel its heat lick my neck. My cheeks.

"Pick your next words," I tell him slowly, "very fucking carefully."

Nico takes in a breath.

23

NICO

*I*t's nine years ago, and I'm in Chrys' powder-blue childhood bedroom.

We fall into her bed, and the second our backs hit the mattress, we burst out laughing.

"Good Lord," I groan. "Your family is...something."

Chrys lifts her eyebrows. "You think?"

We're both dressed in our Thanksgiving best—Chrys in an auburn pantsuit that matches her hair, while I'm wearing a grey blazer and slacks. I wanted to look like I belonged to her; after all, that is the ruse.

Her parents—the hyper-traditional people that they are— have been begging for her to bring a boy back home ever since she started college. So, this year, she asked me to appease them.

I cherish Chrys more than I cherish the breath in my lungs. If she asked me to jump, I'd say *off what?* When I first met her, she was soft and shy and afraid of her own shadow. Now, she's bold, vibrant, and unapologetically herself in a way that has made me utterly addicted to her. I didn't have to think twice about her offer: I was going to be there for her, in whatever way she needed me.

With dinner over, we now lie side by side in her room, staring at the ceiling fan above us.

"Do you think they fell for it?" I ask.

"Fell for it? I think they fell for *you*." Chrys snorts on a laugh. "If I don't marry you, I think my father will."

"Well, he is quite handsome. I see where you get it."

I get a pillow to the face for that comment.

When I toss the pillow to the side, however, I notice that Chrys is staring at me. Her ginger hair is fanned out on the mattress underneath her, and those sea-green eyes are locked on me curiously. "Are you calling me handsome?"

I reach out and trace my fingertips over her cheekbone. "Incredibly."

She wets her lips with the tip of her tongue. We both know what's going to happen next before it happens—there's an agreement, an electric shift in the air.

Chrys leans over and places her mouth gently on mine. I cradle the back of her head and return the kiss. It's sweet, and somehow familiar, the way we explore each other with our lips and tongues.

It's the first time we've kissed, and yet it somehow feels like we've done this before.

And perhaps I have practiced this. In my fantasies. In the quiet hours when I allow myself to want my best friend.

She climbs into my lap and straddles me, her hands on my chest. I'm aching for her, an ache that runs straight from my groin to my heart.

"Don't make a sound," she whispers against my lips, and I have to bite back a whimper when she slips her hand underneath my trousers.

24

NICO

"*Y*ou had *sex* with her!"

Eric is shouting now. Eric is unhinged.

I, on the other hand, am a lake without ripples. I weave my fingers together and rest them calmly in my lap as he paces back and forth in our tight bedroom.

"Once. Many years ago."

"And you didn't think to mention it?"

"It was irrelevant."

Eric makes a sweeping motion with his hand. "She's playing my fiancée—I'd say it's pretty goddamn relevant."

My lips thin. "Just because you're my boyfriend doesn't make you privy to my entire sexual history."

"Don't give me that holier-than-thou bullshit," Eric snarls, and he's right up in my face now. "I'm not talking to the fucking pope. I'm talking to my boyfriend."

"So *talk*. Instead of...whatever *this* is."

His jaw sets. He swivels around and storms out of the bedroom.

Oh no...

I follow after him. He plants his feet and says simply, "You."

74

Chrys is in the kitchen. She's hunched over what's left of the bread pudding. She looks startled, eyes wide, and she drops her spoon, palms up. "I don't know how the bread pudding got here."

"I'm not talking about dessert. I'm talking about my boyfriend. What game are you playing?"

She squints. "Game?"

"Enough, Eric," I tell him firmly. I plant both palms on his chest. "No one is conniving against you. Take a breath. Look at me. Why are you mad?"

He's fuming. Like a bull in the red. "You know why."

"Because you're possessive of me? Or...perhaps you're possessive of her?"

His jaw sets, but he doesn't look at me. "Don't."

But I continue. "Or is this a flare-up of Eric North and his pervasive need to be the center of attention?"

The look Eric gives me could end my life. He steps back and slams the bedroom door. I hear it lock behind him.

"Well," I say. "That was charming."

"Did I...do something wrong?" Chrys says. She's still wide-eyed and confused.

I sigh. "No, dove. Not in the slightest."

I stand beside her. My heart feels impossibly heavy.

"Perhaps it was a mistake to come here," I say.

She looks sympathetic. She holds up a spoon. "Bread pudding?"

"Yes. I think I should."

We carve up the rest of the pudding in silence.

25

NICO

I wake up to the sound of the front door shutting. I'm in Chrys' bed. She's soft and comfortable beside me.

I'm in the same clothes I wore last night. Carefully, so as not to disturb her, I lift myself out of bed and exit the bedroom, quietly closing the door behind me.

Eric has just come back from a run. He's sweating through his sweatshirt, AirPods in his ears. He plucks them out when he sees me, tucking them into his pocket.

"Good morning," I tell him. I fix my glasses on my face.

He crouches to unlace his sneakers. "Get packed," he says. "We're leaving for Spain."

"*We?*"

Those blue eyes meet mine. "Yes. We. The three of us."

"I don't think so." I fold my arms over my chest. "I'm returning home."

"You've only been here a night."

"Yes. And you've made it very clear that you don't want me here. So I'll be out of your hair. I'll see you when you get back to LA."

"If that's what you want."

We're both short with each other this morning. Curt. But at least he's lost the roar in his voice.

Eric removes his shoes and his socks. Then he pulls his sweatshirt over his head.

His torso gleams with sweat. I want to lick the salt from his body. I want to inhale his must.

I tighten my arms around my chest.

"It's not what I want," I insist. "But it's what is necessary. If I stay, we'll make each other crazy."

Eric pushes his pants off and his briefs, casually undressing in front of me as though it's the most natural thing in the world. My throat tightens with want. His body is perfectly sculpted and so masculine—the thick hair at his chest, under his armpits. My gaze can't help but fall to the impressive length of him. Even soft, he's so big, and it makes my mouth water.

Those steel-blue eyes meet mine. "Am I making you crazy?" he asks.

I want to retort, but I can't. The words won't come out.

He leaves me standing there, vanishing into the bedroom but leaving the door open. An invitation.

I hear the shower hiss.

My pants have gone tight, and I am throbbing in them.

My conviction is strong. But I am weak for him.

I follow him into the bedroom and close the door behind me. I undress before stepping into the bathroom. He's turned it up hot, and the steam fogs my glasses immediately. I remove them, setting them on the sink.

My vision is blurry when I step into the shower. Somehow, my lips find his anyway. His kiss claims me, hungrily parting my mouth with his tongue.

"This doesn't mean I forgive you for the way you acted last night," I clarify.

"I don't want your forgiveness," he tells me. "I want your body."

He turns me around. I brace my palms against the wall. His lips claim my throat as he slides his hands down my sides, pushing himself flush against me. I feel his hardening cock against my ass, and I push my hips back, teasing him with just enough friction to make him groan in my ear.

The both of us are wound tight. He hooks one arm around my chest, his large hand circling my throat. His other hand is slick with soap, and his fingers move between my cheeks before penetrating me. He inserts one finger, then a second, and my throat contracts in his grip when I gasp. My toes curl on the slippery shower floor as he caresses his fingers inside of me, working deep places that make my legs shake.

His fingers slide out. I'm ready for him. The thickness of his cock fills me, and I nearly bite my tongue on a moan.

I need both hands on the wall to brace myself as Eric thrusts, our bodies slippery, sliding together. I pant and fall forward into his embrace as he has his way with me.

This is what I need. I need him to treat me like I'm his. I need to belong to him...and for him to belong to me. He feels good, so good, and when he grunts low in his throat, I shudder.

I'm dripping, so hypersensitive that even the light, tickling spray of the shower on my aching cock feels like it might set me off.

I'm so hard, it hurts.

"Please, Eric," I beg, "Please touch me."

"I am touching you," he murmurs.

I whimper, and my cheeks flush. He knows what I want, but he's going to make me plead for it. "I mean...please touch my—"

But I can't get the rest of the words out, because his grip suddenly tightens around my throat. His fingers constrict, cutting off my air, and my words come to a squeaky halt.

"What's that?" he purrs. "Speak up. I can't give you what you need if you don't tell me."

I'm twitching, throbbing, weeping. And he's getting off on it. He grinds against me, and I struggle in his grasp, trying so hard to speak but unable to get anything out but whines.

He sucks my earlobe, nibbles it, and the sensation feels like it has a direct line to my cock. He runs his tongue along the shell of my ear, and I feel it as though he's licked me from base to tip. I let out a strangled noise as I hit my edge—he hasn't touched me where I need him most, and yet I'm ready to burst.

"Hmm," he murmurs. "If you can't tell me what you want, you must not want it badly enough."

I could cry. My ache is so deep, and still he continues to punish me.

And there's nothing I can do about it.

Worse—I love it.

I love being his. I love his torment. I love needing, even when I'm pushed to the brink of madness like now.

Then Eric lets out a moan, and it's a low-throated, lusty sound, and I know he's reached his edge too. The sound vibrates through me, and my body twitches, humping nothing.

"I'm going to cum," Eric tells me. "And I want you to cum with me."

Finally, he releases his grip on my throat. I choke on hot, wet air. His fingertips graze my chest, my abdomen, and finally wrap around my cock.

The sound of relief that leaves my throat is close to a sob.

I've collapsed against the shower wall, half-bent, my forehead and forearm on the cool tiles. I grip his arm for something to brace myself on, and I feel his corded muscles flex as he jerks me, mercilessly wringing pleasure with every rough stroke.

"Eric!" I cry out, and he grunts hotly in my ear. We both

spill over—him, buried inside of me, me, twitching in his palm, coating his fingers. He sucks marks into my throat, and I mumble a low string of nonsense: words like *oh God* and his name, over and over. He kisses my neck, my back, between my shoulder blades and pumps me until I have nothing left to give him.

We breathe together, slowly coming down from the impossible high. He releases my spent organ, pulls out, and holds me instead. I lean back against him, blissed-out, letting the warm shower pelt little beads of water against my chest and shoulders.

Finally, here, in this sacred space where we're both spent, Eric murmurs in my ear, "I am sorry for how I acted."

"I know." Water beats against my face. "I'm sorry too. I should have told you."

His lips suck my throat. "Come to Spain," he says. "Please. I want you there."

I sigh. "I'm not the only one you have to apologize to."

He tilts his head. "Alright. Tell her to hop in here next."

A smile climbs my lips. "You're making jokes again. That's improvement."

"Don't push it."

I twist so I can face him. I cup his head in my hands, and we kiss. He's warm again. My Eric.

"Je t'aime, mon coeur," I murmur against his mouth.

His lips hitch downward. "I don't speak French."

I nuzzle against him. *"Je t'aime, je te déteste, je suis à toi."*

He pins me back against the wall, and we kiss until the water loses its heat.

26

CHRYS

I've always been a meddler.

Mom used to chastise me about it. *Poke your nose where it doesn't belong and someone's going to chop it off,* she'd say.

Which is a weird thing to say to a child. As though our neighbors walk around with hedge cutters, chopping noses indiscriminately.

But it's always been my nature. I read too many Nancy Drew books, and the thing is, I just couldn't leave a mystery alone. Plus, I like helping people. I'm not the kind of person who can walk away if I see someone on the ground.

I help them up. It's just the way I've been wired.

But when I wake up to an empty bed, feeling like I've swallowed a stone, even I've got to admit: maybe Mom's right. Maybe I flew a little close to the sun on this one.

Eric is pissed. Nico is upset. And perhaps I've been meddling in things I can't begin to understand.

So I prepare to fall on my sword. I don a powder-blue dress, brush my hair, and apply a light layer of eye shadow to widen my eyes. Then I take a breath and exit my room.

I'm prepared to be greeted with pitchforks and a guillotine. Instead, there's a platter of pastries on the black marble kitchen counter.

"Good morning," says Nico from the chaise, book in hand.

"Morning," I repeat. "Did you guys get breakfast?"

"I had it brought up." Eric stands by the french press and asks, "Coffee?"

"Sure." I feel like I've stepped into an episode of *The Twilight Zone*. Last night, they were at each other's throats. At *my* throat. Now, Nico is happy as a kitten in a pile of yarn, curled up with his book, and Eric is smiling. *Smiling.*

"Sorry," I come out with, because I'm nothing if not blunt, "I feel like I skipped a chapter."

Nico puts his thumb in his book and folds the pages. "I think I'm going to read on the patio for a bit," he says. "Don't mind me."

With that, he exits the double doors and sits on the porch, overlooking the cobbled streets.

I turn to Eric, eyebrows raised.

He presses his fingertips to the countertop and turns to face me. His lips have thinned, and it reminds me of the face of a child on his way to the principal's office.

"I'm sorry for how I acted last night," he says, clearing the air. "I got angry. I took it out on you."

My mouth falls open.

An apology? From the granite man himself?

I guess I should be grateful. Instead, I feel my own temper start to rise.

I fold my arms over my chest. "Apology considered. Do you want to talk about it?"

The edge of his mouth twists. "Nico told me about how you two..." He finishes his sentence with a sweeping gesture.

My eyebrows climb my forehead. "How we...*what*?"

"You know. Engaged. Intimately."

"*Sex? That's* what that was about? Jesus, that was almost ten years ago—I thought you knew!"

He lets out a short sigh. "I reacted poorly."

"Look—I don't know what you think I am. But I came as a favor to Nico. Believe it or not, pretending to be engaged to you hasn't exactly been the time of my life. I don't know if you've noticed, but you're kind of an asshole."

The edge of his mouth twitches.

"Yes. I guess I am."

"Do you have to guess?"

"You're a good friend," he says.

"I'm a *great* friend," I correct sternly. "And a great fiancée. Frankly, you should be kissing my feet. Not yelling at me in the middle of the night."

"You're right." He steps forward and crouches down in front of me. I watch as Eric slips his hand over my ankle, tilts down, and presses a small kiss to the top of my foot. His grey bread scratches, but his lips are soft.

He glances up. Those blue eyes are dazzling.

I'm not going lie. Seeing him on his knees in front of me sends a strange, unexpected heat through my blood.

"Better?" he asks.

I can't help the grin that plays on my lips. I shrug. "It's a start."

His expression falls. Clearly, he's used to things coming easy to him.

"What can I do to make it up to you?"

I pout and tap my lips, pretending to think. "*Well.* There is one thing…"

* * *

"Odysseus' son. Also a street in New Orleans. Ten letters."

"Ah!" Nico says. "I know this! Telemachus, son of Penelope and Odysseus. A tragic story too."

The plane rattles. I'm squished between Eric and Nico. I lean on the fold-up table to scratch the letters into the crossword puzzle. Sure enough, they fit. "Bingo! That's ten points for Nico, seven for me, and Eric rounding us out at whopping *one*."

Eric scowls. He is, I've learned, a sore loser. "How the hell do you two store so much useless knowledge in your head?"

"It's not useless," I tell him, wagging my pencil. "It's good for crosswords. Here's the next one: stubborn, hardheaded. Four letters."

"Eric," Nico says, and we both laugh.

"I don't like this game," Eric grumbles and pushes open the blind.

"Holy cow," I say.

Nico leans over my shoulder and squints at the crossword puzzle. "No, I don't think that fits."

"No, I mean...*look*."

I point out the window. We're flying over crystal-blue water, the houses that boast beautiful splashes of bright color.

Spain, here we come.

27

ERIC

I drop Nico and Chrys off at the hotel. We're staying in the center of it all—a busy hub in the middle of Madrid.

My agent only booked one room, one bed. I check my watch. I don't have time to sort this out, so I put my card down and drop off my bags. We'll figure out the sleeping arrangements later.

They get to explore the landmarks: Palacio de Cristal, a glass palace conservatory in the middle of a lush park, and Museo del Prado, which houses Rembrandts, Raphaels, and a couple other of Nico's favorite artists.

Meanwhile, I work. I've got an interview with a morning show. It doesn't go great—I need a translator most of the time, and I find myself sorely wishing I brought Nico.

They send me a picture of the two of them posing in front of the golden lions in front of the Cibeles Fountain, however, and my heart soars at that.

I survive the interview, unscrew my fake smile, and go back to the hotel. Just enough time to shove some food in my mouth before Nico and Chrys come bouncing through the

85

door like a couple of cats who just smoked ten pounds of catnip.

"Dibs on the bedroom! I'm getting changed!" Chrys shouts and races to the bedroom.

"Ten minutes!" Nico calls after her.

They whirligig around me, and I set my plastic bowl of hotel salad on the counter before someone knocks it over.

"*Hola, mi amor*," Nico purrs and winds his arms around my shoulders. This city (or maybe it's Chrys?) makes him vibrant in a way I don't normally get to see from him. He's grinning ear to ear, and his dark beard brushes mine when he comes in for a kiss. "How did your day go?"

"Fine. Not as much fun as yours."

"Yes, well, that's about to change. We're going dancing."

I lift my eyebrows. "Dancing?"

"Yes! All three of us. We met this very charming man—he runs some of the tours at Museo del Prado—and he recommended a spot just outside the city for dancing. He called it a local treasure. We must go."

"You met a charming man?" I put my hand under his chin, taking him by the jaw and forcing him to look at me.

Nico grunts, but his eyes light up. He likes it when I get possessive of him. Which is good, because I like possessing him.

"Yes. And if you don't want me to meet any more charming men...I suggest you join us." He slips his hands over my chest and adds, "Wear something looser, my darling. You look incredibly...*stiff*."

He leans into me and punctuates his last word by wedging his thigh between my legs.

He's not wrong. I am throbbingly stiff.

"I'll get changed."

"Ten minutes," he repeats with a wink.

* * *

Our cab rolls us over cobblestone streets and winds us around houses the color of parrots, stacked along the cliff-side facing the long stretch of ocean. The water blushes under the sunset, a low, burning red and orange.

I roll down the window. The weather is nice here. Brisk but warmer than Paris, with a hint of that ocean salt.

I've dressed down in a black button-up that I've opened up at the chest and cargo shorts. Nico and Chrys have gotten into the spirit—his shirt has bursts of red flowers, her dress blends in with the sunset.

The cab drops us off at a small hole-in-the-wall. The double doors are open, and a few people loiter around outside, smoking and drinking and chatting. The three of us slip inside, and I avoid eye contact—I'm not in the mood to be noticed. Inside, the bar is at half capacity, and the salsa music is loud. Nico takes Chrys' hand and spins her as I order three *cervezas* at the bar.

At the bar, we run into their "charming" tour guide from earlier. He's tall and bronzed, and he touches Nico on the arm when they talk.

I wouldn't mind hitting the guy.

Instead, I linger at the bar.

"Aren't you going to dance?" Chrys asks, sidling up beside me. Her hair has come undone, and it sits at her shoulders in bountiful curls.

"I don't dance."

"You must know *some* moves."

"I can waltz. I had to learn it for a part."

"Okay, so just do *that*," Chrys says, "but move your hips."

She puts her hands on my hips and draws me away from the bar toward the center of the room, where everyone has congregated to dance. Her body moves like water—rolling and swaying in a way that's hypnotizing.

"See?" Chrys says, grinning. "Life is better when you relax."

"Relaxing is bad for my health."

She slips her arms around my shoulders. She smells like sweet flowers and honey. I find myself leaning into her, matching my movements to hers.

But my eyes keep catching on Nico and Mr. Charming.

Nico's gaze flickers to the two of us on the dance floor. He smiles, then turns his attention back to the other man.

A terrible, sordid part of me wants to take my fake fiancée and fuck her against the wall just to get Nico's attention.

The song ends, and Chrys hoots. She's having a great time. I take a swallow from my beer. It goes down too smoothly. We head to the bar for another round.

"Hey!" Three young men approach us, smiling. "I recognize you!"

Here we go.

I press on a tight grin. "I'm not doing autographs right now, sorry—"

But then one of the men points at Chrys. "Tuna girl!"

"Oh! Yes!" Chrys hops over and wedges herself between two of the guys, flinging her arms around the both of them. "You want a selfie? Say Tu-Naaah!"

They all put on cheesy smiles as one of the men angles his phone to take a group selfie.

I feel Nico before I see him. He slips behind me at the bar, elbow leaning on the table, and lets out a soft sigh.

"Ah, look at our girl. All grown up and doting on her fans."

Our girl. Why does that phrase make my cock swell?

The bartender has been ignoring me. I lift my empty and beckon with it to get his attention.

"Having fun with your man?" I ask.

"Having *conversation*," Nico corrects. "Having fun with your fiancée?"

My beer finally arrives, and I tilt it to my lips instead of answering him.

I get distracted, however, when I hear a collective groan from the three men surrounding Chrys.

She's trying to peel away from them, but they want her to stay. They want her to party with them. She laughs, keeping her charm, and politely declines. But when she turns away from them, one of the men reaches out and smacks her on the ass.

Oh. Fuck no.

I see red.

In two seconds, I'm in the middle of the crowd. I grab the twentysomething by the front of his shirt, lift him, and force him back against the wall.

His shell necklace jangles, and his eyes go wide.

"Apologize to her," I snap at him.

"Eric! Eric, it's okay." Chrys is by my side suddenly, and she puts her hand on my arm. Then I hear her whisper in my ear, "Please. People are watching."

My heart is roaring. I want to snap this man like a toothpick.

Instead, I take a breath. Force some of the venom out of my blood.

I drop him. Quickly, he stammers, "*Lo siento, señorita.*"

"Perhaps we should leave," Nico says, appearing on my other side. He's my calm in the storm, his voice unmoved. It brings me down a level.

The three of us escape the bar before anyone can whip out their cell phones.

28

CHRYS

*O*ur night out is…eventful, to say the least.

But hey, is it really an adventure without a bar brawl?

Eric is quiet on the ride back to the hotel. Brooding.

Nico fills the silences, but I can't just ignore the fact that Eric North went from Casablanca to Rambo in less than a second.

When we get back to the hotel and back to our room, I decide to clear the air.

There's a small bar set up, complete with two stools, and I claim one of the stools and start taking off my earrings.

"Look…as much as I appreciate the knight-in-shining-armor act, it wasn't that big of a deal."

Eric's eyebrows climb his forehead. "Not that big of a deal?"

I shrug. "It's okay. It happens all the time."

Now Nico comes around and sits down beside me. "How often is all of the time?"

"I mean…" I lift my hand, drop it. "Hollywood is full of sharks, right? I'm used to it."

Nico and Eric exchange a glance, and then Nico asks, "What sharks, exactly?"

"You know. *Sharks*. Like my agent, Roger Bartlett. He's..." I tuck in my lips as I try to figure out how to phrase this next part. "You know, one of those casting couch creeps. Every role has to be *earned*."

Eric's sharp blue eyes examine me. "What exactly does he have you do to earn your roles?"

I tuck my hair behind my ear. This part is embarrassing, and I feel weird confessing it. I've never told this to anyone. I shrug, eyes on the floor, and try to act casual about it. "Just...*stuff*. Sexual stuff, sometimes. I get that that's just how it is in Hollywood, but—"

But then Nico puts his hand on my leg. His chestnut eyes look intense and earnest.

"That's not okay. You understand that, right?"

Something about the tone of his voice...it makes my throat pinch with some emotion I didn't realize I was holding back.

I can't reply. Instead, I just shrug.

Nico sighs. "You're an actress. Yes? Let's do a little role-playing. Consent 101." He puts his hands on my shoulders and adjusts me to look at him. "I'll set the scene. We're at a bar, you're all alone, and I'm a complete stranger. You can only say *yes* or *no*. Understood?"

"Alright...I mean, *yes*."

"Good." He gets up, walks away, then comes back and motions to the chair next to me. "*Hola*, beautiful. Can I join you?"

"Yes."

"Wonderful." He takes the seat beside me. "Can I buy you a drink?"

I can't help the grin that climbs my face. "Yes."

"Bartender!" he snaps at Eric. Eric casts him a sharp look

but then takes a role that suits him well: the surly, moody bartender.

"Can I help you?"

"Yes—a glass of merlot for myself and this stunning woman beside me. Thank you."

Eric—to his credit—plays the role he's been allotted. He takes two glasses from the top of the minifridge and sets them up on the counter in front of us. He pours us each a glass of water.

Nico's chestnut eyes gleam from behind his glasses. "I've been watching you all night. The way you dance. I knew if I left without saying something to you, I'd regret it for the rest of my life."

Oh, he's smooth. I bite my lip against a smile in response. Eric pushes the two glasses over to us. Nico takes his room key out of his pocket and slides it over. "You can start a tab."

Eric takes the card and sets it on the minifridge.

Nico takes the glass and tilts it. "Cheers." I click my glass against his. The water is cold and nice on my throat.

Nico slides his hand over my thigh. "Is this okay?" he asks.

"Yes."

"I know I'm forward, but I'm very drawn to you." His hand rubs up the bare skin of my thigh. I feel myself start to grow hot. His fingers are so long, and despite myself, I wonder what they might feel like inside of me.

He touches the side of my face then, drawing me toward him. I fall into those soft brown pools. He ghosts his thumb over my bottom lip and says, "Can I kiss you?"

My breath catches in my throat. "Yes…"

A sly smile draws over his mouth. He nestles his nose to my cheek, and I feel his breath on my face. "You know," he says softly, "the point of this exercise is that you have to say *no* at some point."

Right. I snap out of it. I put my hands to his chest and halt him. "Sorry—no."

"Ah, I see." Nico peels back into his own chair, wrapping his hands around the glass. "I'm sorry, I misunderstood."

Just then, Eric breaks into the scene. He takes a towel and pretends to be wiping the counter in front of me. "Is this man bothering you, miss?" he asks me.

I can't help but bite on a grin. *Oh, this is fun.* "Yes."

He frowns. Then he takes the room key and tosses it across the table back at Nico. "Your card's been declined," he says.

Nico blinks. "Oh. Well. Try it again."

"No." Eric glances over at me. "You're going to have to find another way to pay for your drinks. You can start by making it up to this young woman."

"Ah. Well." Nico looks flustered, trying to keep up now that Eric has gone off script. "I'm sorry—"

"Not good enough," Eric counters. He looks over at me and says, completely serious, "Would you like this guy to get on his knees and kiss your feet? I haven't mopped the floor in weeks. Should serve him right."

It's taking everything within me to hold back my laughter. They are having *way* too much fun with this. And... honestly? So am I. I play my part. I swivel my chair toward him, straighten my back, and extend a leg toward Nico, toes pointed in invitation. "Yes."

Nico wets his lips with the tip of his tongue. He adjusts his glasses on his face and then slides down onto his knees in front of me. Gingerly, he frees the strap of my heel from its clasp and slides my shoe off, setting it to the side. He takes my naked foot in his hand and grazes his lips over the top of it.

His eyes meet mine. There's a shift in his expression. Those brown eyes are soft and warm. It's as though getting on his knees has flipped a switch in him, and now he's gone completely submissive for me.

For us.

"Is this okay?" Nico asks.

"Yes," I reply, and I'm surprised at the breathiness in my own voice.

The sight sends a rush of burning heat between my legs. I'm uncomfortably wet, and I squeeze my thighs together, trying to discreetly relieve the pressure.

He presses a kiss to my instep, and his fuzzy beard tickles lightly, making my toes curl. Then his lips find my ankle. He presses sweet, worshipping kisses up my leg, and it makes my entire body buzz.

"He's an obedient boy," Eric says behind me, his voice this low, velvet thing. "Isn't he?"

"Yes," I murmur. I slip my fingers through Nico's dark, curly hair. He leans into my touch like a puppy.

"Can I touch you?" Eric asks. My mouth goes dry at the thought.

"Yes."

His fingertips graze the back of my neck, making me shiver. My skin goes tight, and I can feel my nipples harden underneath my dress. He takes a handful of my hair in his hand.

His grip goes tight. Suddenly, in my mind's eye, I see a flash—I'm in my agent's office, and he's got his fingers in my hair, pushing me down.

I put my hand over Eric's. "No," I tell him. "No hair pulling, please."

He relaxes his grip instantly. Immediately, I'm safe again. He moves his hand to my throat instead and caresses his thumb over my jaw. "How's this?"

I tilt into his touch. "Yes. Better."

Asking for what I want—and getting it. How novel. How hot.

"Can I kiss you here?" he asks. His breath is hot on my ear.

"Yes...please..."

Eric's lips claim my throat. Underneath my ear. Meanwhile, Nico's kisses work their way up my second foot, over my legs. I'm covered in their affection—head to toe, literally.

I find myself gasping. I lean back into Eric's kisses, and my legs shift apart, wanting.

Suddenly, Eric growls in my ear, "Do you want Nico to lick your cunt?"

His words vibrate through me. I bite my lip on my answer.

I want it. I want it more than anything. But am I *allowed* to have it?

This space feels safe, somehow. I feel safe here, between these two men. Safe enough to be honest about what I want.

Finally, I say, "Yes..."

Nico slides my panties off my legs.

I should feel vulnerable. I don't. Instead, I feel horny as hell, and powerful.

He nestles himself between my thighs. His breath is hot against my wet sex. He teases me first with soft, gentle kisses, and then his tongue parts my slit.

I moan. I collapse back into Eric's arms and hook a leg over Nico's shoulders, my heel in his back. Nico licks his way up and down my slit, learning me. His tongue presses inside of me, and he sucks and nibbles my oh-so-sensitive skin. When he finds that little bundle of nerves between my legs, I gasp, and my legs start to shake. He zeroes in on the spot, swirling his tongue right there.

Eric rests his hand over my throat. His grip is strong, and I feel safe in his arms. "He's a very good boy," Eric murmurs. "Isn't he?"

Nico moans at the praise. The sound vibrates from his lips over my cunt and makes me shiver. "Yes," I breathe.

"He's good with his tongue," Eric continues.

"Yes," I gasp. I curl my fingers tightly into Nico's hair, and he moans again. Each lick sends hot bolts of pleasure through me, and I can't stop the words from flowing from me. "Yes...yes...*yes!*"

Eric pants at my ear. "Do you want to cum for him?"

My thighs lock around Nico's head. I'm trembling. I can't hold back. "Yes! Please!"

"Let go," Eric growls. "Now."

I shout. My orgasm nearly blinds me, it's so intense. My fingers dig into Nico's hair, and I grab Eric's arm, holding the both of them to me. Nico lets out a soft noise of encouragement as he laps me, eagerly catching every pulse with his tongue. I'm sure my nails are leaving marks in Eric's forearm, but he only holds my throat and nibbles my ear, coaxing me through the throbbing pleasure with "That's good. Good girl. Keep going."

It seems like it will never end. I crest the waves as both men draw me out until I have nothing more to give. My thighs are shaking uncontrollably when I finally whimper, "Please, I can't..."

"That's enough, Nico," Eric says, and his word is final.

Nico stills his tongue. He presses a last kiss to my aching nethers before gently untangling himself from my legs. He stands then, and he hovers in front of me, his hands resting on my thighs.

And then, reality sets in:

I just came.

On the lips of my best friend from college.

While his boyfriend whispered filthy encouragements in my ear.

This is either the best or worst moment of my life, and I can't decide which just yet.

For a moment, no one says anything. We just catch our

breath, the electricity of what we've just done humming in the air like a lingering perfume.

"I need to reset," Eric says, finally breaking the tension. "I'm going to get some wine. Do you need anything else?"

Both Nico and I respond with "no" and "thank you."

Eric draws away from us. He takes Nico's "credit card,, aka the room key, and exits the room.

For a second, Nico and I stare at each other. The air is softer without Eric in it.

Nico's eyes are bright, vibrant. "How do you feel?" he asks. His voice is gentle, genuine.

I squint at him. "You've got some of *me* on your face."

His beard is positively glistening with me. At that, he grins. "I suppose I should wash up."

"Same. I think I wrecked the chair."

He laughs at that. His laugh makes *me* laugh in turn.

Whatever tension was in the air has popped. We're normal again. *Us.*

He extends his hand in offering. "My lady."

I take his hand as he dramatically helps me out of the chair. True to word—the seat cushion is *soaked.* Whoops.

The two of us slip into the bathroom. Nico's hair looks wild, and my panties are on the floor. I go to the toilet to wipe off my pussy (I'm so wet, it's insane), and Nico rinses off his beard and face at the sink.

"So what just happened…" I start. "Was that…okay?"

"How do you mean?"

"I mean…I know Eric can be…uh—"

"Moody? Possessive? Capricious?"

I turn my palm upward beseechingly. "I just don't want to…rock the boat."

He smiles. "I understand that you are shy about saying no. Eric and I are not. If he were uncomfortable—or if I was—we would have said something."

I get off the toilet and readjust my dress around my hips.

"It's just...you two are so crazy in love. I don't want to...get in the middle of anything."

"You won't." Nico steps forward and catches my chin in his hand, trapping my thumb under his bottom lip. "Unless you...prefer it. The middle."

I can't help the grin that spreads across my face. "Why did we ever fall out of touch?"

"Because everything happens when you need it to happen."

I let out a small hum at that. I link my fingers in his. "It's possible you're the healthiest relationship I've ever had."

His eyebrows furrow at that. He looks at me intensely through those sweet brown eyes. "You deserve better than what you've been given. You know that, don't you?"

I give his hand a squeeze. "I *have* better. I have you."

His gaze softens at that. "Can I kiss you?"

"Yes."

His lips meet mine. It's the sweetest kiss I've ever tasted. Loving. Adoring.

I *adore* this man. And he adores me.

29

ERIC

$\mathcal{I}$ haven't slept with a woman since my freshman
year of college.

Even then, it was a forced thing. A last-ditch effort to tell
myself I wasn't gay.

But, suddenly, it's all I can think about.

Chrys' pitchy moans. The sweet, sharp scent of Chrys'
arousal. The way she seemed to fall apart when she came,
crashing down between us.

I want to make her cum. Again and again.

What the hell has gotten into me?

There's a small general store on the corner. I grab a
chilled bottle of champagne and a box of condoms and don't
make eye contact with the seller.

The truth is, it's more than the fact that Chrys is a
woman.

It's the fact that Chrys isn't *Nico*.

Nico is, and has always been, fluid about his sexuality.
Open. He's told me about relationships he's been in before
us. Some of them open. Some of them poly. Threesomes.
Foursomes. To him, sex is something to be enjoyed freely,
not coveted.

Me, I'm old-fashioned.

Monogamous. Single-partner. The end. When I'm with someone, I'm with *them*. They own me. Mind, body, soul.

So wanting Chrys feels like a betrayal. Even if Nico doesn't see it that way.

It doesn't matter. *I* know better. Me.

It's a betrayal against my own nature. Against my better judgment.

I go back to the hotel and punch the button for the elevator and wait.

I can put an end to this. I can go upstairs, give Chrys the bottle of champagne, tell her good night, and fuck my boyfriend's brains out.

It'd be that simple.

But as I get in the elevator and let it take me up, I know:

I can't shove this one under the rug. This is a loose thread, and the longer I avoid it, the more unraveled I'm going to feel.

So as I stand outside of the door that leads to our hotel suite, I make a conscious, purposeful decision.

Whatever I do tonight, from here on out, will be because I want it.

Not my agent. Not the public. Me. Eric.

I can't hide from this. I can't pretend it's someone else's fault.

Every step I take will be a mark in stone. Whatever the outcome, it will be my decision and mine alone.

There's freedom in decisiveness. I exhale. I enter.

The living room is empty. I see the empty glasses on the kitchen counter. Chrys' chair, the navy fabric lightly stained.

But no sign of them.

"Hello?"

"We're in here," Nico's voice calls out. It's coming from the bedroom—our bedroom.

I cross the living room and follow his voice. They're in

bed. Nico's shirt is gone. She's in her nightshirt—no pants, those long, bare legs lazing across the bed.

The sight of the two of them like this—warm, soft, and just a little devious—makes my mouth dry.

"Daddy's home," Nico muses. He has a mischievous look about him that makes my blood hot.

"Yes," I state. "He is." I kick off my shoes and socks and set the bag down before I crawl into bed. "Have you kids been good while I've been gone?"

"Yes, Daddy," Chrys says sweetly.

I'm so hard, I can't breathe.

"Why do I feel like that's a lie?" I pinch Nico's nipple and flick it. He gasps sharply.

"We were just...ah...getting comfortable..." He stumbles over his words.

"I see that." I put my hand on his chest, pushing him to his back and pinning him there. I'm in my element now. In control. I nibble his throat. His muscles twitch. "So there was no kissing while I was gone?"

"There...may have been a little bit of that, sir," Nico gasps. He's squirming, aroused, *mine*.

"That's what I thought." I take the back of his head and close my mouth over his then. He's wonderfully familiar. I know every crevice of this man's mouth; I know the fuzz of his beard.

When we break away, Nico clings to me and murmurs softly in my ear, "It's okay to want her. I give you permission."

And then...

A switch flips.

Fuck it.

My gaze turns to Chrys. She's shy, keeping to her edge of the bed.

I take her face in my hand. One more sanity check. "Is this okay?" I ask.

101

Those emerald-green eyes flicker over me. "Yes. Is it okay for you?"

The question of the hour. Answer honestly.

I brush my lips against hers, testing. "I want you," I tell her in no uncertain terms.

She meets my kiss.

She's not familiar. Her lips are so soft, her skin so smooth. Her kiss is sweet and gentle, and when her tongue caresses mine, it's timid. Exploratory.

The sweetness of her is going to give me a heart attack.

I cup her face and touch my thumb to her bottom lip.

"Do you want me to fuck you?" I ask.

"Eric, I—"

"No," I interrupt. "Call me Daddy."

Her lips part in a small *oh*, and I see her eyes immediately brighten.

She and I are the same. We're more comfortable when we're wearing masks.

"Please, Daddy," she purrs. "I want you inside of me."

I reach over the side of the bed, grab the box of condoms, and pluck one out. I hand it over to her. "Then be a good girl and put this on."

She bites her lip excitedly. I've slotted myself between her legs, and I rise to my knees. Her fingers make quick work of my button and slide the zipper down on my jeans.

My need is vulgar. I'm already bulging out of my briefs. She slips her hands in my pants and caresses me through my briefs.

"Oh," she says softly. "You're hard."

The innocent way her fingers explore makes me shiver.

"The two of you make me crazy," I say.

I lock eyes with Nico. He's sitting up against the headboard, watching us.

"Enjoying the view?" I ask him.

He wets his lips. "Very."

His chestnut eyes are alight with lust.

Chrys pushes down my briefs and—thank God—wraps her fingers around my cock. I don't realize how pent-up I am until the relief of her touch is so intense, my breath catches.

She bites her lip. *Shit*. The way her teeth pin that plump lip makes me harder than I thought possible.

"Can I make a confession?" she asks as she tears open the condom wrapper. "Full disclosure: you might hate it."

I chuckle. "Now's as good of a time as any."

"So…I had a minor crush on you in high school. Well, not *you*, you. Dr. Wolfe."

I nearly choke. *Dr. Wolfe* was my character from a cheesy medical soap opera. Wolfe made it two seasons before dying of a broken heart.

Again. It was dumb show.

"Your age is showing," I tell her. I was in my midthirties during filming. She was in *high school*.

She shrugs and slides the condom over me. It's been a while since I've worn one of these, and it's slightly sticky as it rolls on. "I had a TV in my room. It came on every evening at five thirty. I may have…uh…humped my pillow a couple times to that show."

Jesus Christ. Normally, I don't care for fans. But her confession is making my heart pound.

"You're sick," I tell her.

She blinks at me. "I am?"

"Yes. I'm diagnosing you as a kinky little girl."

A smile breaks over her mouth. She tosses her head back dramatically, the back of her hand on her forehead. "Oh, Doctor, will I ever be cured?"

"I hope not."

I put my hand on her chest, pin her down against the mattress, and claim her mouth in my own. She sighs softly in my mouth, and her legs wrap around my hips.

"Nurse," I say, eyes catching on Nico's, "lend a hand."

Nico scoots over and sits cross-legged, drawing her head into his lap. He pets her hair back, running his fingers through her long, ginger strands. She leans back into his caresses, eyes falling closed, enjoying it.

"Let's see..." he says thoughtfully. He runs his hand down and rests it at her chest. "Your heart is beating very fast."

I push out of the rest of my clothes. Together, Nico and I strip Chrys—he tugs her shirt off, I pull her panties down. Then he slides his hands over her round breasts and lightly pinches her nipples. She gasps and giggles in surprise.

"Responsive to stimulus," Nico says.

I reach between her legs. She's so soft here, like silk, and she's slick with arousal.

"Oh, God," Chrys whimpers as I push a finger inside of her.

I have large hands, strong fingers, and with only one finger in, I can already feel her tight around me. She's so hot, and she blushes as I work my finger inside of her, exploring her. I ease a second finger in, stretching her, and she gasps and rolls her hips upward, taking me in to the knuckles.

She's ready.

I remove my fingers and nestle my cock between her legs instead. The tip kisses her tight entrance, and with a thrust of my hips, I sheath myself completely inside of her.

"Oh!" Chrys cries out in Nico's lap. "Fuck! You feel so good..."

Nico caresses her hair and plays with her tits. "Good girl," he murmurs to her gently. "You're doing so well..."

Even with the condom between us, I can feel her sweet heat.

She's so open to the both of us. Brave in her vulnerability. It's...incredibly arousing.

I feel animalistic. I grab her thigh and thrust into her, again and again.

I want to make her scream. And I do.

Her hand clings to my chest, nails digging into the hair and skin there. The other hand clings to Nico's thigh, grounding her.

Nico holding her down gives me perfect leverage to pound into her, exactly how I want it. It's not long before I feel her legs begin to tremble around my hips.

"God," she says, and her emerald eyes flicker between me and Nico, her expression something close to panic. "Oh God, I think I'm going to cum again—"

I can feel it. The tightness of her. The way she pulses around my cock.

"Beg," I demand.

Now there's *real* panic in her eyes, and I know she's afraid she won't be able to hold off. "Please," she whimpers. "Please, Daddy—"

That does it. I grip her thigh, fuck the ever-loving hell out of her pussy, and growl, "Come for me, baby."

She screams when she orgasms. She clings, her body throbbing around me.

I'm close.

I need Nico.

I grab Nico by his hair and pull him in for a rough, sloppy kiss. He opens to me, inviting me into the warm cavern of his mouth.

I come undone on his lips. Inside of her. Tangled up in the both of them.

I cum so hard, I feel turned inside out.

I rock into her a couple times more, muffled moans on Nico's lips, clutching the back of his neck. It's not until I'm drained and she's melted into tiny, quieter pulses that I finally still my hips.

I break my kiss with Nico to tilt downward and catch her lips. She's so warm, so lazy, like she just woke up from a long night's rest.

We collapse, limbs tangled. Panting. For the first time in

days, I feel like I can breathe. My marionette strings have been cut, and for a moment, it's just me, Chrys, and Nico. I don't have to pretend. I don't want to be anywhere else but right here, right now.

"That was..."

"Amazing," she finishes.

Her emerald eyes sparkle at me.

She's so sweet. So perfect. My heart hurts.

I kiss her again. I've fucked her roughly. Now, I'm gentle with her.

I kiss Nico as well. And then I kiss his jaw. His throat. I press my kisses down his body, and my fingers pop open the button on his pants. I can feel his erection straining the fabric underneath.

But then Nico rests his hand on my wrist, stopping me.

"No, please," he says. "Not tonight. I want to live in this for a moment."

I understand. Nico doesn't always crave orgasms. Sometimes, he only wants closeness. Intimacy.

"I guess we don't have to figure out the one-bed thing anymore, huh?"

I can tell Chrys is trying to be strong, but when she asks the question, her voice trembles a little.

If we send her to the couch now, it'll break her heart.

Personally, it would break *mine* too.

That's not an option. Not even remotely.

I reassure her by catching her chin between my fingers and tilting her head to look at me. "You're not going anywhere," I tell her. "You're staying right here. Understand?"

She nods, and I can see the shimmer in her eyes. "Thank you."

My body is relaxed, and my cock has softened inside of her enough that I can pull out and roll the condom off. I've filled the damn thing, and I climb out of bed and go into the bathroom to dispose of it and wash the stickiness and cum off myself.

When I come back, Nico and Chrys are completely wrapped up in each other. Arms and legs tangled. Snuggling like a puppy pile.

Jesus. My heart feels like it might expand right out of my chest at the sight.

I climb back into bed beside Chrys and press a kiss to the top of Nico's head and then to her shoulder. "Look at you two," I murmur. "Perfect angels."

"There's room for a devil," Nico says, holding out his hand.

I slide in beside Chrys and wrap my arms around the both of them.

I'm so content, sleep hits me like a sack of bricks. I'm knocked out before I know it, lulled by the warmth of their bodies and the soft sounds of their breaths.

30

NICO

$\mathcal{I}$ wake up in a cocoon of warmth.

Chrys is cuddled up on my chest, her hair tickling my chin. Eric is wrapped around her, his hand on my side.

Watching them sleep, I couldn't be more content. My heart swells in my chest.

Last night was something magical. I'm sure of it.

Chrys was an angel. Beautiful. A vision when she lost control.

And then there's Eric.

He's so peaceful now, tangled in both of us.

I touch his head, tracing my fingers through his greying hair, but he doesn't stir. He sleeps like the dead. When was the last time he was able to sleep without Ambien? It's been so long, I can't recall.

I needed this. *We* needed this.

I haven't felt this close to him in a very long time.

I want to fall back asleep with them and savor this. But my body clock won't let me. Once I'm up, I'm up. So I gently extract myself from their warmth. I removed my pants to sleep, but I'm still in my boxers, and I fumble for my glasses and my phone. I use the light on my phone so as not to wake them and guide my way through the maze of clothes on the floor and into the bathroom.

I'm in the middle of brushing my teeth when there's a knock on the door.

"Come in," I say.

It cracks open, and Eric is on the other side, wearing bed head and his briefs. He also has his flashlight on his phone.

"Good morning, devil," I tell him.

"I have to piss."

"Be my guest."

If you can't urinate in front of each other, is it truly a relationship?

He finishes and sidles up next to me to wash his hands.

"How do you feel?" I ask casually.

"Tired."

"I mean...about last night."

He focuses his gaze on his hands, running them longer through the water than necessary. "Satisfied," he says finally. "But..."

"But?"

He turns off the sink, then turns to me. Seriously, he says, "I don't need anyone but you. I need you to know that."

Oh...

I put my toothbrush down, spit in the sink, and turn my full attention to him.

"I do know that. But you *want* her. It's okay." I put my hands on his shoulders and squeeze. "I want her too. And I loved seeing you together."

I nestle against him. Here, I feel his rigid posture soften. His shoulders drop a little, relaxing, and in this safe space, he confesses, "She...unlocks something in me."

"You have a type."

"Yes. Male."

"No," I reason with him. "Doe-eyed. Damsel in distress. You like to be the hero."

Eric lets out a small laugh. "The hero. I like that."

"You certainly saved me." I put my forehead to his. We're intimate like this, and I savor the moment. "Scooped me out from the bottom of my pool like a prince."

"I'd do it again in a heartbeat, puppy."

Puppy. The way he says it makes my knees weak.

"I like the way you look at her," I tell him. "It's different from the way you look at me."

"How?"

"You're very…gentle with her."

His eyebrows knit. "I'm not gentle with you?"

"No." I ghost my lips over his. "Because you know I can take it."

Those sapphire eyes flash. My wolf, temporarily sated, is now hungry again.

"Come here," he says, and the firmness of his tone doesn't give me a choice. Neither does the way he grabs my chin and tilts it so he can kiss me—hard, wanting.

I sigh into his mouth.

Eric doesn't waste time. He reaches between us and cups his hand over my groin. He massages me over my boxers, and my needy cock springs to life.

"I have been cruel to you," he murmurs in my ear. "Look at the desperate state I left you in."

His tongue catches my earlobe, and he gives it a small tug between his teeth. I shudder. My cock aches, and I want so badly for him to touch me.

"Yes," I whisper. "I need you terribly."

He plucks the elastic of my boxers and tugs them down, freeing my erection. There's moisturizer on the counter, and he drops a dollop in his palm before smearing it over my cock. His hand slides easily up and down my shaft, and I shiver in his strong grip.

110

The tip of his tongue traces my ear. His teeth meet my neck. "Whine for me, puppy," he growls. He sucks my throat, pulling the blood to the surface, and I whine loudly.

The jolt of pain makes my cock leap in his hand. I can't help myself—all the ache from last night had compounded my lust, driving me insane. I find myself pushing my hips forward into his hand, rutting against him.

He chuckles lowly at that—a sound that makes my heart pound. "Look at the state of you, puppy. Humping my leg. I'm going to have to train you better."

He gives my cock a gentle squeeze, and the tightness of his grip makes my eyes roll back. Already, I feel my muscles tense, preparing for the impending, rocketing orgasm.

"Do you know how much I love you like this?" he murmurs. "Throbbing in my hand? It's my favorite fucking thing in the world."

I bite my lip against a moan.

Suddenly, the counter starts to buzz. It's Eric's cell vibrating.

I gasp and look at him fearfully. I'm so close. I want so badly for this to keep going.

With his free hand, he checks the caller ID. But his other hand remains wrapped around me. Eric glances at me. I can see the gears of his brain working.

"It's my agent. I have to answer this."

I'm so frustrated, I could cry.

But instead of pulling away, he nips my bottom lip and gives my aching cock another squeeze. "Don't cum. Understand?"

The commanding look in his eyes takes my breath away. "Yes..."

He answers his phone, putting it to his ear. "'Lo?"

But his gaze remains fixed on me. He resumes pumping me, his slick palm sending delicious waves of pleasure through me with every stroke.

111

My breath catches. I want to moan, but Eric is on the phone, so I swallow the noise back. My throat is dry.

"Yes," he continues—and damn him, how can he sound so calm, so professional right now? Meanwhile, I feel like I could shake apart at any minute. "Yes, I know. I've got a car. I'll be there."

His eyes leave my face now. He stares into nothing, distracted, as he listens.

"Her?" he continues. "Is that necessary?"

His touch slows but doesn't stop. Absently, he lingers at the tip of me, rubbing his fingertips over my oh-so-sensitive head.

I don't know if he's even aware of what he's doing. But I'm so sensitive, even the light touch of his fingertips is too much. I yelp before I can stop myself, my body jerking.

Eric narrows his eyes at me. *Whoops.*

He returns his fingers to my shaft and gives me a squeeze. A warning.

I pant, my tongue at the roof of my mouth.

"Hm?" he says. "Oh. Nothing. Just a puppy barking outside."

I bite my lip so hard, I taste blood.

I'm wound up beyond belief. I'm trembling; my blood is screaming.

I'm close. I'm so close. Every stroke of his hand is torment. I can feel myself start to sweat, my body trembling.

Eric's gaze meets mine. I mouth the word *Please*, but his jaw locks and his eyes go hard. He shakes his head.

Don't you dare, his expression says.

There is the promise of punishment in his eyes if I don't follow orders.

My toes curl, and my fingers tightly grip the edge of the sink. I ride the razor-thin edge as he strokes me, lazily. Mercilessly. Pumping me. Ever. So. Close.

"Will do. You too."

Eric finally ends the call and sets his phone down on the counter.

I exhale a breath I don't realize I've been holding, and with that breath, I sputter, "Please, *please*, oh God, I'm so close…"

"I can see that," he says calmly. He crushes his mouth against mine, and I moan into his kiss. He pulls his hand up my cock, to the tip, and I'm certain that, on his downstroke, I'll explode into his hand, whether he gives me permission or not.

But I don't get the chance to find out. Because he continues upward until he lifts his hand from me, letting go of my cock completely.

I whimper. My hips rise, meeting nothing.

"Unfortunately," Eric says (though the rich velvet of his voice tells me he doesn't mean *unfortunately* at all—he's enjoying this too much), "I have to go. I have an interview to catch."

I bite my lip to keep myself from begging.

My sweet, sadistic Eric smiles.

"Be a good boy," he tells me, "and I'll finish this when I get back."

He flicks the tip of my cock once. I choke on a groan. I'm wound so tight that even the smallest touch nearly sends me to my edge.

But more than I want to orgasm…I want to please him.

I love these frustrating games we play, just as much as he does.

"Yes," I say, my voice hoarse with want. "Thank you."

My submission makes his gaze soft. He takes the side of my face in his hand and kisses me once, tenderly.

"I love you," he says suddenly. "You know that, don't you?"

"Yes." I smile. "Always."

"Clean yourself up," he tells me, and with that, he exits.

I am a mess.

A twitching, leaking, aching mess.

I want terribly to finish myself, but I know better. Instead, I take a tissue and clean the precum from my cock (carefully so as not to set myself off). I slip my boxers back on, and even the light caress of the fabric over my swollen organ nearly makes me moan.

I rinse my face off in the sink. Cold water. I'm trying to calm the pounding of my heart.

It's going to be a very, very hard day indeed.

On the other side of the door, I hear Eric talking to Chrys:

"Princess. Wake up. You're coming with me."

CHRYS

I feel like I'm walking through a dream.

No—scratch that. *Last night* feels like the dream. An insane, impossible dream.

Because this morning, we're back to reality.

I'm sitting in the waiting room at a news station, adjusting my dress at my knees, and feeling like I can't get comfortable in this seat.

Playing the role of Eric's fiancée feels...different now, somehow.

Before, it was just a part. An acting gig.

Now...I've reached into the most intimate parts of his relationship. I've seen what he looks like unraveled. I've tasted Nico's kisses and fallen asleep on his chest.

This doesn't feel like *playing house* anymore. It feels...

Unsettling.

Like I'm split between multiple realities, and I can't be sure which one is real.

"Are you sure I'm supposed to be here?" I ask Eric.

He's sitting beside me, dressed in a dashing grey suit and distracting himself by scrolling through his phone. At the sound of my voice, however, he lifts his head and pockets his phone, giving me his attention.

"My agent scheduled the interview for the both of us. She wants people to see us together."

"Right, but..." I chew my lip. "What am I supposed to say?"

Eric cups my face in his hand. I freeze at his touch. He puts his thumb to my mouth and unpins my bottom lip from between my teeth as if it's the most natural thing in the world.

And, I guess, it is. We're supposed to be engaged, aren't we?

"Just relax," he says. "They want to know about the movie. I'll do most of the talking."

An assistant pops her head into our cubicle-like waiting room. "Mr. North? They're ready for you."

But he turns to me first and asks, "Ready?"

I nod. "Ready."

He takes my hand, and the small touch is comforting. We've already been through makeup and wardrobe, and now they pin small microphones to our shirts. Eric doesn't release my hand once, and I let him take the lead. I follow him out of the waiting room, around the set. There's cheery music playing, and when we step onto the stage, an applause track kicks in, even though there's no audience in sight—nothing but bright lights and camera eyes pointed at us.

And we're live.

It's a morning talk show with two couches in an L shape at the center of the room. The host—and namesake of the show—Mauve stands when we enter. She's in a bright purple dress with sky-high blonde hair and so much makeup she gives me Effie from *The Hunger Games* vibes.

She lets out a pitchy squeal when we enter and hugs Eric tight and then gives me a kiss on both cheeks. Eric and I sit on the couch opposite her and settle in.

"First things first," Mauve says and slaps her hands against her neon tights. "Congratulations to the happy couple!"

"Thanks," Eric says. He exchanges a smile with me and takes my hand. The moment seems intimate.

"Tell us—are you two enjoying your engagement?"

"I couldn't be happier," I say, all smiles. Now that we're in front of the cameras, I am feeling myself slowly ease into my element. I'm bright, chipper, excited to be here!

"She's a good girl," Eric agrees and holds my stare a little too long.

His eyes are all smolder, and I can't help but wonder if that charm is meant for the cameras or for me.

To be honest? It's working.

Memories of last night rise to the surface, and it takes everything within me not to bite my lip.

"Chrys Hudson, the girl next door—I want to know *everything* about you," Mauve says. She takes a hold of my hands, pulling me out of Eric's grip, and forces my attention onto her. "You went to Elmswood College, correct?"

"Um…yes. Yeah. For acting. And I've worked a bit since then—"

"You two share a common friend," she interrupts. "Nico Ortega, yes?"

Um…*what?*

Out of the corner of my eye, I see all the color drain from Eric's face. *Where is this line of questioning coming from?*

I laugh it off. "Yeah—yes. I mean, Nico and I went to school together. And then he and Eric did the movie, *Second Hand Kill*, and…actually, that was how Eric and I met—"

I'm blustering, but it's working. I concoct a believable story on the spot, how the three of us met at a mutual gathering and it was *love at first sight* with Eric.

Eric is a stone beside me. He says nothing. His mouth seems cemented shut, his jaw a hard line.

We move off the topic of Nico, I fib around with a couple of wedding plans, and the time whizzes by. Eventually, Mauve turns to the camera and says, "We'll be right back— after the break!"

Immediately, the cameras cut, and we move to commercials.

The air around us is toxic. It's the static electricity right before a bolt of lightning.

"Hey," Eric says, his tone sharp as a knife, "are we going to talk about *Catch & Kill* anytime soon?"

"Yes, of course. After the break." Mauve smiles so wide, all of her teeth show. Her crew comes around and reapplies makeup.

I need it. I've sweat down the back of my neck.

Eric, however, is worse. He looks like he might crawl under the very nice glass table and have a panic attack. Even his breathing has gone shallow, his chest rising and falling lightly.

"Hey." I reach out and take his hand in mine. He's trembling. "Are you okay?"

"Fine," he says gruffly.

I press my lips together. I decide to try something.

"Give me your palm," I say.

He gives me an odd look but relents. He holds out his hand, and I take it in mine, palm up, as though I'm about to do a reading.

"Look away," I tell him. "I'm going to write a word, and you have to guess what it is."

He turns his gaze forward. I use the tip of my finger and draw an *E* into his palm.

He furrows his brow. "Do it again."

I trace the letter again, slower this time.

Now, he gets it. "*E*."

"Yep." I draw out three more letters.

"Eric," he says.

"Bingo. Now try this one."

I trace another word into his palm. As Eric concentrates, I can see him start to relax. All the parts of his brain telling him to panic have switched into puzzle-solving mode. His hands have stopped shaking, at least.

"Chrys," he says.

"You got it. Okay, one more."

I trace the last word into his palm. D-A-D-D-Y.

When it clicks, he smiles. A real smile.

"On air in five!" an assistant chirps, and we put on our masks again.

Mauve finally steers the conversation to *Catch & Kill*. Eric is relaxed now and back in the zone; he answers her questions with his infamous suave. They play a clip from the movie—it's a mid-action scene. Eric and his co-actor are caught in the middle of a firefight. Eric tries to keep the bad guys off their tail, all while engaging in frustrated, comical banter with the other man. It's good. *Fun*. And I watch Eric as he watches the clip. His mouth twitches in a small smile. He's proud of his work—as he should be. It's nice to see.

We end the interview, give Mauve a polite but curt parting, and escape into the back room. Assistants unpin our microphones, and Eric and I set up by the mirrors with swabs of cotton to remove the thick, anti-glare makeup.

"Where did you learn that?" Eric asks once we're alone.

"Learn what?"

"The hand thing."

I side-eye him through the mirror. "You're not the only one with secrets, Mr. Hollywood."

He arches his eyebrows.

I give in. "I used to have anxiety. Like...*severe* anxiety. When I went off to college, it just...took a hold of me. I could barely get out of bed. Started skipping classes. The whole nine. They had those free campus counselors, so I finally bit the bullet and started seeing one. He recommended that I try something to help me get out of my shell.

"So you'd think—start small, right? Nah. I went big. I joined the improv club at our school, even though I'd never been an actress before. But it was all about...trusting your gut. Trusting your instincts. Trusting your partner. That really appealed to me. I started to get more comfortable in my skin. More confident. That's actually where I met Nico."

Now, I have Eric's full attention. Those blue eyes stare at me, quietly listening.

I continue. "He'd already been in the class for a year, so he helped me learn the ropes. We'd practice a lot together. I felt safe with him. At the end of the class, we had this big end-of-semester show. The audience was small—we had maybe fifty people there? Maybe less? But the day of the show, it was like all my panic came rushing back. I didn't think I'd be able to go out there.

"So Nico sat with me backstage. We did a couple exercises to take my mind off of things. And then he had me turn around, and he'd start writing words on my back. Any words. Dog. Flower. Something to take my mind off of my fear. I remember the last word he wrote was *brave*. It felt like he was branding the word into my skin...writing it into my bones. So I took that bravery with me, and I went onstage."

"How'd the show go?" Eric asks.

"Oh, terrible! We got some real stinkers of reviews. But you know what? I didn't care. It just felt *so good* to walk onstage and claim my place in the spotlight. After that, I switched my major to acting and never looked back. I kept going to therapy, landed an agent, and...the rest is history."

Eric, to his credit, listens to me. He just listens. Those blue eyes are sharp and thoughtful.

Finally, he sets down the cotton and turns to me—not mirror-me.

"You never got your Parisian breakfast," he says. "I think I owe you one."

I can't help but grin. "I'd like that."

32

NICO

I get a text to meet the two of them at a café near the hotel.

I find them at an outdoor table. It's a beautiful, historical café with blue stone walls, a wide courtyard, and gas-lit lanterns. The tables are marble, the chairs sea green.

We order beef sirloin taquitos, roasted eggplant with honey, and *patatas con nuestra brava*. It's barely noon, but Eric orders champagne for the table.

"Are we celebrating?" I ask.

"Yes," he says. "We're celebrating the weekend."

"It's Wednesday."

"My weekend. I have two full, interrupted days until my next appearance."

I can tell by his expression that he needs this break. Interviews always take it out of him, but he looks particularly worn.

"Two days," Chrys muses as she dices up her eggplant. "What do you want to do?"

"Let's go somewhere," Eric says. "Anywhere."

"Anywhere is a big place," I inform.

The waiter comes around and asks if we need anything.

Eric asks for a pen and paper and does a bad job miming the words, so I translate for him. He comes back with a notepad, and Eric thanks him.

Eric takes a page out and then starts ripping the paper into small strips.

"What are you doing?"

"You take three," he says, handing three strips over to me. "And you." He gives a handful to Chrys as well. "Each of you write down three places you want to visit. Somewhere within a couple hours by plane, preferably. We'll pull out one, and that's where we go."

"Where are yours?" Chrys asks.

"I don't care where we go. As long as we *go*."

I take the pen, consider my options, and then write them down. I hand them back to Eric, and then Chrys does the same. She's all grins, and I admit, this *is* quite fun.

Eric crumbles them up into small balls, then puts them in his palm. He cups his hands together, shakes, and then makes an opening at the top with his thumbs and holds his hands up toward Chrys. "Lady's pick."

She plucks a ball out and unravels it. Her eyes light up.

"We're going to Bruges!"

Eric looks surprised. He glances between the two of us. "Whose pick was that?"

"Mine," I say, just as Chrys echoes the same word.

Eric lifts his eyebrows. He dumps the balls onto the table and unfurls each of the remaining five crumpled slips.

Sure enough, among the suggestions for *Rome* and *Athens* are two requests for *Bruges* in Chrys' and my handwriting.

"Birds of a feather," Chrys says.

"You two are so goddamn cute," Eric says candidly. "I want to spank you both until you cry."

Jesus. Is this…*my* Eric? The way he comes out with something so filthy, so casually, over *brunch* of all places, makes my breath catch in my throat and my cock stir in my pants.

Yes, he's been this vulgar before. In the shadows. In the privacy of our own home.

But here, he's bold. Confident. It's a good look on him.

I can tell his words produce the same effect on Chrys. Her cheeks go red, but she can't hide her smile.

"Alright," Eric continues, "Bruges it is."

33

CHRYS

*J*t's already late when we land in the glittering city.

As we drive from the airport to the hotel, I feel like I've entered a fairy tale. We pass medieval-style houses with pointed roofs and old brick with climbing ivy. Charming canals with willow trees kissing the water. Signs with insane Dutch words that seem to stretch on for miles.

Eric has booked a small cottage for us that overlooks one of the canals. There's a pocket of similar cottages nearby, all run by the same stout innkeeper, who speaks English and was able to talk with Eric at length as Nico and I got settled.

Most importantly, this place is *private*. I like that about it. It feels like the three of us have our own little bubble here.

Anything's possible in a fairy-tale land. And with the three of us in this blissful little honeymoon stage of...*whatever* this is...it's nice to have the freedom to explore outside of prying eyes and paparazzi.

This would be a good time to stop for a second and think about the fact that I fell into bed with my best friend...and my fake fiancé.

But, honestly?

All I can think about is how safe Nico makes me feel.

And how much I enjoy the predatory glint in Eric's eyes.

Like the way he's looking at me right now. Nico is in the shower. I've parked my makeup kit on a desk that faces the window so I can look out the river while I get ready. I stole the small vanity mirror from the bathroom and propped it up next to the window. As I attempt to detangle my hair (which is thick as a wooly mammoth), I catch Eric's eyes in the mirror.

He's already ready. Dressed in tan pants and a navy blue shirt that matches his eyes. He sits on the velvet living room couch, and his eyes have locked on me.

It's that *wolf about to eat Little Red's grandmother* look.

I can't help the smile that creeps up my face. "Can I help you?"

Those deep blue eyes don't leave me. "What are you doing?"

"Detangling the rat's nest."

"Come here. Bring your brush."

I get up from my seat and come over to him. I hand over the brush, and he says, "Turn around."

Okaaaay. I turn and feel him pop me once on the ass with the back of the brush.

"Ow!"

"Does that hurt?"

Yes…and no. I was caught off guard at first, but now my skin tingles pleasantly in the spot where the brush hit me.

"Not in a bad way."

He smacks my other cheek with the hard back of the brush. This time, it makes me gasp.

"Sit," he says. "On the floor."

I fold my legs underneath me and lower myself to the floor between his knees. Eric's large fingers run through my hair, pulling it back over my shoulders. I close my eyes as the teeth of the brush tickle my scalp. He's gentle with the knots,

126

holding my hair at the root to detangle them, making every effort not to hurt me.

It's soft and sweet, and the top of my head feels massaged with each pass of the brush.

"You have beautiful hair," he murmurs. The tone of his voice is low, dreamlike.

"Thank you, Daddy," I whisper.

For once, I'm not trying to turn him on with the word. And, for once, he doesn't pounce on me. Instead, we've both fallen into a tranquil space: he's taking care of me, and I've opened myself up to let it happen.

I could exist in this space forever.

Eric says, "I want you to know…when this started, I didn't know what to think about you. Hell, I didn't even like you very much."

I snort on a laugh. "The feeling was mutual."

"I didn't give you a chance. And now that I have…I care about you. A lot."

I tilt my head fully back and rest it against his thigh so I can look him in the eyes. I gasp dramatically. "Eric North… are you…*talking* about your feelings?"

A smile twitches at the edge of his mouth. "Don't get used to it."

I clasp his leg and give a little squeeze, encouraging. "Why do you care about me?"

He goes serious at that, his mouth thinning. "You have a big heart. Like Nico. You're honest. Brave. I respect you for that."

"I like this. Keep going."

"I like the person I am with you. You make me…soft."

My eyes flick from his face, to his groin, and back to his face. "I don't make *all* of you soft."

He lets out a light laugh. "That's not what I meant." He runs his fingers deep into my hair, and my eyes fall closed.

My lips part. The feeling is orgasmic. Eric continues. "You make me gentle. I want to take care of you. Protect you."

Then he leans down and presses a small, chaste kiss to my forehead.

I hum contently. "For the record...I care about you too."

I feel his smile on my skin.

"Are we ready?"

I open my eyes and see Nico standing in the open bedroom doorway. He looks sharp in tight pants and a loose button-up. He looks clean, warm, his dark hair still wet from the shower.

"Just about," Eric says and releases me from his grasp. He sets the brush down on the table in front of us. "I have a couple things to wrap up, then I have to get on a call with Monica. You two go ahead—I'll meet you there."

* * *

Nico and I get to the restaurant ahead of Eric.

It's within walking distance of our stay, which is nice. We don't have long here, and I want to take it all in.

Nico extends an elbow, and I hook my arm in his. We walk side by side to the restaurant and then take our table, sitting across from each other. Dutch is one of the few languages Nico *isn't* fluent in, but together the two of us fumble through the menu.

We order drinks and a couple of appetizers. As we wait, we lapse into a small silence. I notice Nico's gaze fixes on my hand.

He's staring at my engagement ring. I feel a strange jolt of guilt.

I twist the ring on my finger. "Is this weird for you?"

He blinks as though waking up from a reverie. A smile creeps across his face. "No. Perhaps what's weird is how unweird it is."

I splay out my fingers so I can admire the rock. "Eric said you picked it out."

"Yes. Ruby. Your birthstone."

"I can't believe you remembered that."

"I remember everything, darling."

In his eyes, I see a hint of something else.

Everything. Like that night we both shared tangled up in each other's bodies. That night he made me whimper in my childhood bed.

That everything.

The memories make me bite my lip in a smile.

"I remember everything too," I tell him. I bump my foot against his.

I want to kiss him. I want to feel the softness of his beard against my face. I want the familiarity of his lips. I even want that awkward moment when his glasses get trapped between us.

But instead, I settle for playing footsie under the table and Nico's soulful eye contact.

Eric returns to the table. He sits across from me, beside Nico, and tucks his phone into his pocket.

"Sorry that took so long," he says. He looks serious, so I keep my feet to myself.

"Is everything okay?" I ask.

He nods, then looks up at me. "My agent wants to meet you."

I blink. "Me? Did I do something wrong?"

"No, not about…this. She wants to represent you."

I open my mouth. Close it. Try again. No sound comes out.

My heart is trapped in my throat, making it impossible to speak.

Eric continues. "It's not a guarantee. She still wants to see your reel. Your resume. But I spoke to her, and she has the availability. She's willing to take you on if you want it."

Finally, my brain comes back to me. I'm able to force out the words "I have a contract with my agent—"

Eric shakes his head. "Chrys...this is the big time. That contract is pennies to her. If she likes you, she'll have no problem paying the cost to break it. It's an investment to her."

I shake my head. "I don't know. Roger—"

Eric puts his hand over mine. "You're not going to work for that man ever again. Do you understand? He doesn't own you. He doesn't get to put his hands on you."

My vision blurs. The restaurant, Nico and Eric—all of it becomes a rust-and-gold blur in front of me. My throat constricts, and I can barely catch my breath.

I try to take a sip of water, but my hand shakes, spilling ice down my dress.

"I'm—sorry," I fumble, using the napkin to brush the water off. "I'll be right back."

I can hear Nico call my name. But I can't stop. I can't break into tears—not here.

I rush through the restaurant, barely aware of where I'm going. I find a door to the back patio and push it open.

There's no one out here. It's started to drizzle, and the damp weather keeps everyone inside, the chairs pushed up against the tables.

There are stone steps leading out, and I sit down on one of them. No paparazzi here. I'm alone. In this small, safe moment, I let myself break.

I heave out the enormous sob I've been holding back. It makes my body tremble, and once I start crying, I can't stop. I fold myself over my knees and let it all come out—buckets of tears, masked under the patter of rain.

It feels *good* to cry. It feels good to crack open and let it all out.

I'm not alone for long, though. I hear the door creak open

and shut behind me. I don't have to lift my head to know who's behind me.

Nico rests his palm lightly on my back. "Chrys." He murmurs my name so gently that it pulls another sob from me. "What's wrong?"

I try to pull myself together. I push the heel of my palm against my face, smearing my tears, and sniffle.

"It's amazing," I manage to get out. "It's...it's what I've wanted."

"*But?*" Nico presses.

My bottom lip trembles. I look down at my feet and whisper, "I don't deserve it."

"Yes. You do."

Nico wraps his arm around my shoulders. He pulls me against his chest, and I'm so comforted here. So safe. He presses a kiss to the top of my head and murmurs into my hair, "Darling, you deserve the world."

CHRYS

$\mathcal{E}$ventually, I stop crying enough to pull myself together and go back inside. Eric asks if I want to leave, but I don't—I want to stay here and celebrate with these two.

We order wine and cheers. *To new starts.*

As dinner goes on, I feel my tears dry on my cheeks, and my shoulders lighten. It's like a minotaur has been riding piggyback on my shoulders, and finally, the monster has stepped off. I can breathe. By the end of dinner, I'm laughing so loudly, the other tables look at us oddly.

We get back to the rental, and I feel like I'm on cloud nine. It gets brisk here at night, and Eric lent me his blazer for the walk back. It's big on me but warm and cozy. Once we're inside, I shrug it off and hand it back to him.

"What now?" I ask.

"Now," Eric says, "you both change into robes and get in bed. I have a surprise coming up."

Nico and I exchange glances, then grins.

We race into the bathroom. We take off our clothes in front of each other. It strikes me how incredibly unshy I am around him.

Three robes hang from hooks by the door. I slip into mine. It's a perfect fit. Soft silk.

"How do I look?" I ask, dramatically sashaying.

"Luxurious," Nico purrs.

We both climb into bed together.

There's a knock on the door. "Are you two decent?"

"In body, not in mind," Nico replies.

The door opens just a crack. "You both have been very, very good. And you've earned a treat."

Why does that make my heart beat faster?

Hello, praise kink!

The door opens the rest of the way, and, lo and behold—Eric pushes in a dessert cart. The cart is stacked with goodies: a large bowl of vanilla, pink, and green ice cream. A bowl of fresh, plump strawberries. House-made whipped cream. Topping, sprinkles, waffle cone pieces. And to top it all off... Eric opens the top of a kettle. Chocolate fondue.

"Okay, it's official," I say. "I've died and gone to heaven."

"Just don't tell my trainer about this," Eric says.

"Darling, I don't think we're telling *anyone* about this," Nico adds, amused.

Eric takes a bowl from a tier below the cart and stands with a scooping spoon in hand. "Alright, Chrys," he says. "What will it be?"

"Oooh, so this is full service?" I press my lips together, examining all my options. "Okay, this is going to take a minute..."

I make him mix together a full bowl of vanilla and mint ice cream, topped with colored sprinkles, tiny marshmallows, hot fudge, and whipped cream.

Basically, I put both the boys' bowls to shame.

Eric climbs into bed finally, and I'm wedged in the middle. I'm cuddled and cozy and savoring the most decadent ice cream on my tongue.

It reminds me of being a kid. Sleepovers with my friends in middle school. It's been so long since I felt safe like this.

There's a big, wide-screen TV across from the bed, and Eric hands over the remote. "Lady's choice," he says.

"Alright. Dr. Wolfe it is."

Eric nearly chokes on his spoon. "Anything but that."

I settle on one of my favorites, *Runaway Bride*. It's a classic, and the three of us laugh over Julia Roberts' antics and comment on what a fox Richard Gere is.

I have the eating habits of an overgrown child, and when a laugh catches me off guard, I manage to spill the contents of my spoon over my chest. "Oh, crap—"

Ice cream slides under my robe, down my chest. "Pass a napkin, please?" I ask, holding out my hand.

"Why?" Nico counters. He parts the top of my robe, and his head dips. His warm tongue slides over the top of my breast, cleaning up my mess.

My nipples start to knot. *Oh.*

Eric watches us, and I see a shift in his gaze. Those bright blue eyes darken with desire as an idea takes hold. He puts his own bowl on the bedside table and holds out his hand. "Puppies shouldn't be eating out of bowls. Give me yours, Nico."

Nico blinks, then obeys, handing his over. Eric takes it, then says to me, "How still can you be?"

I think I know where this is going, and I shiver at the thought. "Pretty still."

His large fingers work the knot of my robe. He parts the sides, fanning them out like wings beside me. I'm stark naked now. Vulnerable.

Eric starts with a small scoop of ice cream. "Try not to make a mess," he says as he puts the dollop on my belly. I don't breathe, trying to keep it from sliding off me. But it's cold, and the ice cream is soft, and I feel it start to melt down my sides.

Nico's eyes are soft and submissive. He looks at Eric and waits, patiently.

"Go ahead," Eric instructs. This time, Nico removes his glasses, putting them to the side. He props himself on his hands and bows over me. His tongue is so gentle, carefully lapping at my stomach. The dual sensations—cold ice cream, hot tongue—make my breath catch.

"I, um, I think I'm done with this," I say, holding out my bowl. My desire for ice cream is strong—but my desire for Nico's tongue is stronger. I want to enjoy this.

Eric looks amused and clears my bowl as well, setting it to the side. Then he takes another spoonful and drizzles it over me again, this time on my thigh. The ice cream is getting melty now, and Nico has to work quickly to lick it up so it doesn't hit the mattress. His hot tongue works up and down my leg, in the crease of my thigh, and I clench.

I'm burning up. My pussy aches to feel his tongue.

"Now," Eric says, "stay very, very still."

As if he can read my mind, the next spoonful…goes right on the top of my thigh. Slowly, I can feel the cold cream trickle down…between my legs and…oh God…*inside*…

I bit my lip and try to keep still. But it's hard. It's so cold, and my body is burning so hot.

Nico's lips kiss my thigh first. He cleans me with his tongue and then moves downward, nestling between my legs. When his tongue finally tastes my swollen nether lips, I can't stop moaning.

"Good boy," Eric murmurs, and Nico lets out a small pleased hum, his lips vibrating on my sensitive skin.

Eric slips his fingers through Nico's hair, petting him, and his ice-blue eyes fix on my face. I'm vibrating with pleasure, each lash of Nico's tongue sending me to new heights.

"Enjoying yourself, princess?" he asks.

"Yes, Daddy."

He tries to hide it, but I can see the way that word makes him shiver.

It's crazy, but—

I like the way Eric *wants* us.

It's primal. Animal.

The way those blue eyes gleam is intense.

So maybe I bite my lip a little harder. Moan a little louder. Spread my legs a little wider so he can better see what he's missing.

Maybe I want him chomping at the bit to get to me.

It works, because he tilts my head and presses his thumb into my mouth. "Open," he commands. I do, parting my lips, extending my tongue. Wanting.

He kisses me. Hard. His tongue swipes over mine, greedy for me.

I feel completely consumed. Nico's tongue between my thighs, Eric's tongue between my lips. Both making me squirm. I'm twisted up in pleasure, and my legs squeeze around Nico's head as they start to tremble. I can feel myself pulsing, tightening, reaching that burst of ecstasy, when—

"That's enough," Eric commands. His voice is a low, rough growl.

Nico pulls back his tongue, so now I can only feel his hot breath panting on my wet sex. I whine in frustration, my body a live wire.

But Eric cups my face in his hand and presses his thumb to my bottom lip, centering me. "Are you still hungry?" he asks me.

"Huh?"

He motions to Nico. "Come here."

Nico climbs up the bed on all fours. Eric pulls him close and kisses him. I love the way they look together—how Nico melts on Eric's lips. Eric removes Nico's robe from him and lets it fall to the bed, then guides him to sit up against the headboard.

"You're a chocolate girl, aren't you?" Eric asks me. I nod.

Eric reaches over to the cart and opens the pot. He dips two fingers in the chocolate fondue. Then he paints it over Nico...his abdomen and up his hard, thick cock.

Nico gasps, and I can tell he's struggling to stay still as Eric's fingers tease him.

"Enjoy," Eric tells me as he sucks the remaining chocolate from his fingers.

I don't waste time. I climb over Nico and position myself between his legs. I start on his abdomen, cleaning him with small, quick flicks of my tongue. His muscles tense and shudder underneath me.

Normally, I don't have a dominant bone in my body. But making this beautiful man shiver...*does* something to me.

I take my time, slowly working my way to the place I know he needs me most. By the time I've licked his stomach clean, his erection is straining, beet red with longing.

Finally, I lavish attention on him there. I work my tongue from the base of him all the way to the tip. He's salty here, and the combination with the sweet chocolate is delicious.

Nico sighs with relief and moans as I suck him down.

He's big, and I can only take him so far. I grip the base of him stroke him as I suck instead. The reaction is lovely. He gasps, and his fingers sink into my hair.

"Oh God, yes, Chrys," he sighs. "That's so good..."

His words send a shot of pleasure through me, making my cunt clench. I work him with my hand, my lips, getting sloppy with want. I hear him gasp, and he whines out a warning. "Please...I'm close..."

"Stop," Eric says suddenly. "He hasn't earned it yet."

I pop him out of my mouth, even though I don't want to. His cock is wet and slick, throbbing in my absence, and I want nothing more than to feel him explode between my lips.

Nico's eyes are hazy. "I don't know how much more I can take."

Eric catches his chin between his fingers. "Do you want to find out?"

"Yes, sir."

"Are you going to be a good puppy for me?"

"Yes..."

"Puppies can't talk. Puppies can only whimper."

He lets out a soft noise, like a whine.

"Good boy. Do you want to fuck her?"

Nico looks at me. Those sweet brown eyes are drunk with lust.

He nods. A shiver of pleasure runs through me.

There's a bowl of ice on the cart, presumably to keep the ice cream cold. Eric plucks an ice cube out of the bowl. "You're very worked up," he muses. "Let's numb you out a bit first. Can't have you having an accident, can we?"

Nico's eyes go wide, but he doesn't protest as Eric slides the ice cube over the length of his hard cock. It looks like glass, leaving a wet trail as he rubs the cube up and down.

Nico's jaw clenches. He hisses and grips the pillow behind him but never once tells Eric to stop.

I love getting these glimpses into their dynamic. Eric is merciless. And Nico?

He loves it.

Nico's angry cock finally starts to wilt under the ice cube. Only then does Eric toss the cube away. He hovers over Nico and takes him in his mouth.

Eric, clearly, has a bit more experience with Nico's monster of a cock than I do. He swallows him down like it's nothing, until his nose touches Nico's pelvis. Nico whimpers, and his heels dig into the mattress as Eric slowly rises, pulling his lips up the length of Nico's cock until he pops free.

"How did that feel?" Eric asks him. "Good?"

Nico nods.

"But numb?"

Nico's face is as red as his erection. He nods again.

Eric rises from the bed. He draws his fingers through my hair as he passes me, and I lean into his hand. I love his small touches, the way he claims us both so effortlessly.

He goes into his bag and pulls out the box of condoms and a bottle of lube. He rips it out of the wrapper, tossing the wrapper to the ground, and comes back, sliding the condom over Nico. Eric takes control, maneuvering us exactly how he wants us. He cups my head, gives me a sweet kiss, and murmurs, "Get on your back, princess."

"Yes, Daddy…"

I slide up on the bed, flat on my bed, head on the pillow. Nico climbs over on top of me, and he nestles against me before his lips find mine.

I sigh into his mouth. I slide my hands down his sides. Where Eric is all hard muscle, Nico is softer. Warmer. I love the way his body feels. I love the gentle heat of this man.

"Is this okay?" he whispers against my lips, checking in with me.

I nod, my blood burning with want. "Yes."

He kisses me again. This time, he presses himself inside of me as we kiss.

I gasp. He's a bit thicker than Eric, and he stretches me when he enters me. I'm so slick with my own want, however, that with one good push he slides in completely. I feel deliciously full, and I wind my legs around his, savoring every inch of him.

I'm so wrapped up in Nico, I don't realize that Eric has climbed on top of us until I hear Nico whine in my mouth. I open my eyes to find that I'm underneath both men—Nico inside of me, Eric inside of Nico.

Nico's pace was slow and gentle. But now Eric grabs his hips and takes control. Nico's cock hits inside of me, hard, and I see stars. It feels *so good*. I gasp, and my hips arch to meet Nico's. Each thrust sends bursts of pleasure deep inside of me. I grip Nico tightly, and his lips meet my throat, my chest—these small, desperate kisses. He's unraveling on top of me, his skin furnace hot and sticky.

My nails must be leaving marks in his hips. My thighs tremble, and my orgasm hits me before I know it's coming. I yelp as I explode with pleasure, throbbing around Nico.

He moans. The motion of their bodies doesn't let up, rocking me through the waves of my orgasm.

"Eric," he murmurs urgently against my chest. "Eric, *please*."

Eric kisses Nico's neck and grips his hair. "Yes, puppy. You can cum."

Nico cries out. His hips jerk against me, and I can feel him pulsing inside of me. He lets out small whimpers, and I can't tell if he's in pleasure, or pain, or somewhere in the middle.

Eric gives a shuddering groan above us, and it sounds like he's reached his peak as well.

For a minute, the three of us just pant. We're sweating, sticky, and I feel sweetly sore and so, so spent.

And then I feel it. A wetness on my chest. Nico's body starts trembling.

I slip my fingers through his hair. "Nico? Are you okay?"

"I'm sorry," he says, his voice shaking. He's crying, though he tries to hide it, and he turns his head to wipe his face. "I'm sorry. I'm not sure what's come over me."

My heart melts. Immediately, I scoop his face in my hands. "Hey," I say, "it's okay... Are these good tears? Or bad tears?"

"Good," he says and smiles softly. "Very good."

I kiss his face gently, his eyes, his cheeks, tasting the salt of his tears. Eric grips Nico's hair and kisses the back of his neck, his shoulders.

"You're a good boy," Eric murmurs. The praise draws another deep sob from Nico.

He's vulnerable right now. Broken up. I can't explain it, but I feel so grateful, suddenly, that he trusts me enough to fall apart with me.

Between the two of us, Eric and I wrap Nico up tightly in our arms and shower him with kisses until he quiets.

"I'm sorry," he says again, once he's composed himself. "That was terribly dramatic of me."

I stroke my hand through his hair. "Don't be. It was intense. Really intense."

Eric has gone quiet now. He leans over and presses a small kiss to Nico's shoulder. "You're safe here," he says, and I believe it.

35

NICO

J wake up reborn.

My body is sore, and spent, and deliciously worn. I feel like taffy, stretched and pliable.

There's an empty space in the bed next to me. I can hear the shower running, a soft hiss from the bathroom.

Behind me, a mountain of warmth. Eric's strong arm locked around me.

The dessert cart is still beside us, the ice cream now a pile of melted goop. The sheets, I'm certain, are a sticky mess.

I make a mental note to remind Eric to tip the cleaners generously.

I shift in Eric's arms to stretch, but he doesn't let me go far. He tightens his grip around my middle and kisses my shoulder. He's awake and probably has been for a while.

"*Guten morgen,*" I tell him. I reach back so I can slip my fingers through his hair.

He nuzzles against my neck. His breath is hot, comforting. "Morning."

Eric can hide from everyone else—but not from me. Even in that single word, I hear something off in his tone.

"Did you sleep well, love?" I ask. Sometimes, the best way to get him to open up is to coax it out of him.

"Mmhm. You?"

"Like the dead."

I pet his hair, those tangled morning curls. We sit in silence for a moment. It's comfortable.

"What's on your mind?" I ask him.

An invitation. Not a demand.

He's quiet for a bit. I think it must help, however, that I can't see his face, because he does finally open up. "I've been thinking about what you said."

"What did I say?"

"That sometimes…I put you through hell because I know you can take it."

"I can."

He exhales. An impatient sigh. "But you shouldn't have to. I ask too much from you."

I twist around in his arms. Facing him now, I can see the pain etched into his expression. This is weighing on him, clearly. Heavily.

I rest my hand on the side of his face and stroke my thumb over the rough stubble along his jawline. "I love you, Eric. Call me a masochist, but I love you."

Those ice-blue eyes bore into me. "You're a masochist."

I smile. "Yes. And I'm willing to do whatever I have to in order to have you." I rest my hand at the back of his neck and look directly into his eyes. *"This,"* I tell him firmly, "is worth everything."

He swallows hard, Adam's apple bobbing. He's doing what Eric always does—pushing down whatever emotions are threatening to break free.

I slide my hand down from his neck to rest it on his bare chest. My palm on his heart. I want him to feel safe here, the same way he makes me feel safe.

"All I want is for you to be happy," I tell him. "You must know that."

He takes my hand in his. He presses it to his lip and gives my finger a small nibble. Affectionate, like a puppy. "You make me happy," he says.

He has a faraway look in his eyes, lapsing into thought. When he returns his gaze to mine, those blue eyes seem clearer. Focused.

"I have my last interview tomorrow," he says. "I want you there."

My heart gives a kick in my chest. He's never invited me to any of his public appearances. I've always been made to watch the replay later on TV. But to see him live, in person, even from the back row?

To catch his gaze in the throng of people, even for a second?

What a treat that would be.

I smile. "Then I'll be there."

He seals the agreement with a kiss, and I melt in his mouth.

36

ERIC

The crowd is ready.

I'm at the last stop of my press tour. London. It's a couple of minutes before the panel, but I break one of my rules and sneak a peek of the audience through the curtain that's separating us from *them*.

They look less threatening when they're not all haloed in bright lights. They're just people. Normal, excited humans. Fans who want to be inspired. Who want to feel, for an hour, like they're part of something bigger than themselves.

Nico and Chrys are here. They're near the front. Nico looks as anxious as ever, tugging at the sleeve of his sweater, glancing around as though someone might kick him out at any moment.

This is it. My last panel. And then it's all over. We can fly back home. Be done with this whole mess.

But I've got thorns in my chest. That ugly, nagging feeling hanging over my shoulder.

You're a liar. A fake.

I find myself twisting my faux engagement ring over and over again around my finger.

"Eric!" I retract from the curtain and glance behind me.

Raul has earbuds in, but he offers me one and pumps at the air. Already, I can hear the chaotic sounds coming from his headphones. "Are you excited? Come! Get pumped!"

"No, thanks."

I don't need him pawing at me. It'll be enough just to get through this.

A crewmember straps a microphone to me, and then it's off to the races.

The cast gets introduced one by one. Each of us gets a resounding round of applause as we take the stage and our seats. There's me, Raul, and the director. We all know our lines. We all know how to sell this movie.

I've played this part a million times. It should be easy. So why does today feel different?

We move to the question-and-answer section of the panel. After a couple of rounds, the interviewer passes the microphone to a kid in the front row.

He's sixteen, maybe seventeen. Tall and awkward. Wearing all black except for the band around his wrist—a rainbow-pattern Pride band.

He hunches even as he stands, like he's trying to hide. Uncomfortable in his own skin. And, fuck, if it isn't like looking through a time machine.

Young Eric North, hating himself, hating his body, hating the things his body wants to do with *other* bodies that look like his.

The kid looks at me, but he can barely hold eye contact for more than a couple of seconds at a time. His smile is lopsided and looks unpracticed, like his face isn't accustomed to the shape of it.

"I…um. My question is for Mr. North."

His voice cracks, and even with the microphone, it's hard to hear him.

I try to encourage him. I nod, lean forward with my elbows on my knees, and say, "Go ahead."

He shifts from one foot to the other. "I wanted to know if...uh. Like. You have anything um...in common. With Colt Carver."

Finally, with the question out, he's able to make eye contact. And those brown eyes—they're so sweet, almost hopeful, and it's fucking heartbreaking.

I take a moment to answer. It's not that I need to consider it—I know what I'm going to say before I say it.

I need a second to gather up the strength to get the words out.

"Thank you...that's a great question," I tell him. "My character...Colt. He's courageous. Bold. Something I'd like to emulate in my life."

I wet my lips and take a breath. Now or never.

I glance at the interviewer and continue. "Which is why I'd like to say something today, if you don't mind."

The interview quirks his eyebrows and then nods. "Yeah, of course."

The truth, Eric.

Say it.

I look for Nico in the audience. He's watching me, curious.

My words tangle in my throat. And all at once, it's *clear* what I need to say.

There are no other options. No other words, except:

"The truth is...I have a boyfriend. I've had a boyfriend. For the past five years. I've kept him hidden because I prioritized my career. I even enlisted his friend to pretend to be my fiancée to keep up the ruse. But I'm tired of lying. It's real. I'm proud of him. And I love him."

I exhale. My chest is tight, but the words are out now. There's no putting them back in.

You could hear a pin drop in the conference center.

Beside me, both Raul and my director have gone completely rigid. Well. *Fuck them.*

147

When I get the courage to look back at Nico and Chrys, I can see they're holding hands. Chrys is smiling—this giant, face-eating smile. Nico's eyes are wet, and my heart pinches in my chest.

They're not the only ones who are happy. There's that kid, still holding the microphone. He stares at me, slack-jawed, like I just handed him the keys to the universe.

And maybe I did. I hope I did.

"Wow," the interviewer says. "That is...quite a thing." He adjusts his glasses and looks at his notes as if that will help him here.

I lift my microphone back to my lips. "Any questions?" I ask, and a hundred hands go up.

37

ERIC

For about thirty minutes, I get grilled about my personal life.

I release information here and there, but I don't go too deep into details. I've relinquished my secret, but I haven't invited the whole damn world into my bedroom.

There are some things that still have to be kept sacred for me and Nico.

I need space to breathe. But I don't get it. I exit the stage, and almost immediately, a volunteer jumps in front of me. "Um. Mr. North?" She holds up a phone. "She says she's your agent. She's been calling...a lot..."

I take the phone. "Hello?"

Monica is spitting mad. "After *everything*," she snarls, "you have the audacity to pull a stunt like that without consulting with me first?"

"It felt right."

"*Right*? You've cost us everything—"

"Monica," I interrupt her bluntly, "either you can represent me as I am, or you can't. There's no middle ground. Your move."

Her voice reaches a pitchy level, but I'm done listening. I hand it back to the shell-shocked volunteer.

"Eric!"

Oh hell, what now?

To my horror, Raul launches himself at me. I brace, preparing for the worst, when—

He smiles and clasps his hand on my shoulder. "I was just talking to Peter. We want you to know, what you did, it's very brave. We have your back, my friend."

And, suddenly, I feel like an asshole.

This man, who is the living embodiment of machismo, is offering an olive branch.

I didn't think it would mean this much to me. But it does. His words hit like a rubber bullet in the chest.

I stick my hand out. "Thank you."

Raul, who still knows nothing about personal space, ignores my hand and squeezes me in a hug instead.

For once, I let him.

This industry will chew good people up and spit them out. It's nice to know I have a lifeline or two in these shark-infested waters.

Even if it is Raul.

He leaves me, and I disappear backstage. There's a small dressing room space, closed off from the rest of the conference, and it's blissfully empty. I tuck myself in there and close the door.

I just need a second. One second with my thoughts.

My heart is pounding. But in a good way—not in the way that warns of an impending panic attack. This feels different. This feels like the high after dropping down a roller coaster. I park myself in a cheap plastic chair and remind myself how to breathe.

I hear the door open and close. A chair scratches along the floor. Chrys sits down beside me and knocks her leg against mine.

"You actors are all the same," she says. "Always a flair for the dramatics."

"Sorry I didn't warn you," I tell her.

She shrugs. But when I look at her, she doesn't look pissed. Instead, she looks pleased, a grin playing on her lips. "I guess the engagement is off?"

"Draw up your prenup."

"Obviously."

She glances down at her hands then. I watch as she twists the ring off her finger and holds it up for me to take. "I guess you should take this back, huh?"

I hold up my palm to stop her.

"No. It's yours."

Her eyebrows knit, confused. "Are you sure?"

I nod. My chest feels tight for reasons I can't explain. "Something to...remember this crazy time in your life by, maybe."

Those green eyes go soft. "Eric, I can't—"

I take her hand, put the ring in her palm, and close her fingers around it. Then I press a kiss to the tops of her fingers. "To the bravest girl I know," I tell her.

Her eyes go wet. She looks like she's about to say something, when—

There's a knock on the door.

Nico enters. Or rather, he hovers. Half in, half out, clutching his elbows. "Sorry. Is this...a bad time?"

"It's a perfect time." Chrys stands, but before she leaves, she leans over and presses a small kiss to my cheek. "Be careful with him," she murmurs under her breath. "He's more fragile than he lets on."

With that, she rises. She goes to Nico and pulls him into a tight hug. They embrace for a minute before she releases him and exits, closing the door behind her.

We're alone now.

I stand. Nico steps closer but keeps a small, polite

distance.

"So," he starts.

"So."

"How are you feeling?"

"Good," I say. "I think."

"Yes." Then his eyes avert. He looks to the floor for a moment before he summons up enough courage to meet my gaze. "Is this my fault?" he asks. "My being here...was it too much? I never wanted you to feel pressured, or—"

"Stop."

"Stop *what?*"

"Stop being so fucking nice."

I close the distance between us. I catch his face in my hand and press a hard, hungry kiss to his mouth. He sighs against my lips, and I feel the shudder in his breath.

Anyone could see us. Anyone could walk out, right now, and see us tangled together. And for the first time, I don't give a damn.

"When I exit," I tell him, "I want you with me. Holding my hand."

He lets out a soft laugh. "I...don't know if I can."

I take his hand in mine. With my thumb, I draw a line down the back of his hand.

"What letter am I writing?" I ask.

He cocks his head. "*I.*"

I draw four more letters.

Nico watches and smiles. "*Love.*"

I write on his skin: Y-O-U.

Nico shivers. He leans in and presses his lips to mine softly. Sweetly.

"Alright," he says and adjusts his glasses on his face, preparing himself. "I'm ready."

I take his hand securely in mine, and together, we walk out into the throng.

CHRYS

*F*elix the Cat swishes above me, his slivers of eyes clicking.

"You won't believe the calls I've been getting," Roger says. I've never seen him this animated. He's swiveling back and forth in his chair, scrolling through his phone with one hand and gesticulating wildly with his other. "Producers. Agents. Reporters. Everyone wants to know who Chrys Hudson is— and they want to ride on the coattails of your notoriety. What'd I tell you? Even bad reviews sell. You're blowing up, kid."

I've worn a dress for the occasion. It's got ladybugs on it, and I like to think I'm channeling all their good luck. Redheads got to stick together, right?

I lean back in my chair and adjust my purse strap on my shoulder. "That's a good thing, right?"

Roger finally looks up from his phone. He looks at me like I'm stupid.

Go ahead, Roger. Underestimate me.

His lips curl in a pity smirk. "Rachel Devon called. She wants you in her next movie. The *lead*, Chrys. This is huge for us."

Us. In your dreams, buddy.

I smile. "Great. Tell her she can get in touch with my agent."

His eyebrows furrow. "She did. Me."

"Oh, no. Not you. You're fired, Roger."

His mouth opens, then closes. Then opens again.

He looks like a goldfish, and I've got to say, a small, evil part of me is relishing the shock on his face.

"What's wrong?" I ask, cooing. "Felix got your tongue?"

Now his face goes red. That was the wrong thing to say, apparently.

"You can't fire me," he hisses. "We have—"

"A contract. I know. My new agent is buying me out, so."

"Your new…" He fumbles on his words. "Who…?"

"None of your business who." I stand. I'm taller than him, like this, and *damn*, it feels good. I put my palm on the desk, lean over to him, and say, "I'm not your business. Ever again."

Now, Roger stands. He hovers over me, trying to intimidate me.

I don't flinch. That pisses him off, and his eyes narrow.

"I think you've forgotten who made you," he says slowly. "You were a trembling, scared little girl when I found you, stumbling over your lines. I got you your first job. I taught you how to act—"

"No," I cut him off. "The only thing you taught me was how to get on my knees."

Boy, he's fuming now. Is a man's face supposed to get that red?

"You ungrateful cunt," he hisses.

I sigh. "Anything else?"

"Yes. You're not the first wannabe to suck my cock for the part, and you won't be the last, so quit crying about it and grow up."

Bingo. I reach into my purse, pull out my phone, and wiggle it between my fingers.

"Wow, that was great. Really Oscar-worthy. I'm sure my lawyer is going to enjoy that recording. I mean, you're really doing his job for him."

For the first time since I've known him, Roger is speechless. He looks at me, and my phone, and back at me again.

But no sound comes out.

"Sucks, doesn't it?" I say. "Feeling helpless."

I should know.

He doesn't respond. He just grinds his teeth.

He knows I have him by the balls. Figuratively speaking, anyway.

I drop my phone back in my purse. Checkmate.

"Well, this was fun. Let's never do this again."

With that, I adjust my purse and turn to leave.

Thank you, ladybugs.

But it turns out I'm not out of the woods yet, because suddenly, I feel a hand grab my arm.

The second Roger touches me, I swirl around and snap at him, firmly. "*No.*"

The single word freezes him in his spot. It feels powerful coming from my lips.

And it works. He retracts his fingers.

I exit swiftly.

I'm not alone. Outside his office, in the small waiting room, Eric and Nico sit side by side on the couch, ready to jump to action if I need it.

I didn't. But it helps to know they're there. And seeing them now feels like the pot of gold at the end of a goddamn beautiful rainbow.

I smile, suddenly feeling spent. "Hey…"

They both stand in sync.

But Roger hasn't quite given up. He's standing in his open doorway now, and he tries out my name. "Chrys—"

Jesus Christ, he's like the villain from a slasher film that just *doesn't know* when to stay down. It's utterly exhausting.

Luckily, my backup takes the cue.

Eric stands between the two of us, blocking me with his body. Between Eric's bulky biceps and cold-as-a-morgue stare, Roger swallows his tongue.

Eric says, slowly, calmly, "Touch her and I'll rip your arm off and shove it down your throat."

Eric, honestly, looks like he could do it too.

Nico comes to me, slipping his arm around my shoulders protectively. He's moving me toward the door, away from the mess that is my former agent. "Are you okay, darling?"

I nod. "I'm fine now. Let's get out of here."

And burn his casting couch to the ground.

39

NICO

*T*hings that make me deliriously happy:
Eating popcorn in bed.

Next to my lover.

Watching our favorite late-night show.

It's been three months since Eric's big announcement, and the best part of it all?

Very little has changed.

Yes, his public appearance has done a three-sixty. *Eric North Gay* trended on Twitter for nearly a week. People couldn't stop talking about his story, about *us*. He's made a couple of statements about it since. He's been working with his agent to coordinate LGBTQ+ advocacy events. Strike while the iron is hot, so to speak, and use his new platform for good.

But with us? We're still wonderfully, blissfully the same.

We can go on dates now. We can hold hands in public. Sometimes, when I'm very lucky, he'll even nestle against my ear and tell me what a good boy I am, and I have to do my best to keep myself from tenting my pants for the paparazzi.

But for the most part, we've simply…slipped back into normalcy.

We have our friends over for intimate backyard dinner parties. We prefer cooking for each other to going out. We make love in the privacy of our own bed, or on the kitchen floor, or in the pool.

There are times when I see the changes in him. He smiles more often. He walks with his shoulders up instead of hunched over. His eyes are brighter, clearer.

He's happier, and I'm happier. But he's still my Eric. My brooding, pain-in-the-ass, introverted boyfriend.

So as much as I love holding hands while we enjoy a candlelit dinner at the Osprey overlooking the coast—I love this more. Being domestic with him. Cuddled up in matching his & his robes, watching our show.

I open my mouth and stick my tongue out. Eric picks up a handful of popcorn and feeds them to me, one by one.

"Ah, this is it," I say excitedly and grab his thigh, giving a squeeze. I point at the television. "Turn it up."

He does. We watch as Chrys enters the screen. She walks on the stage to some pop song, and the crowd explodes as she does a little boogie before taking her seat.

I laugh. The camera loves her, and she owns it. She's incredibly charming.

"She looks great," I say.

"She better." Eric pops a piece of popcorn into his mouth. "I bought her that dress."

"Hush." I give his leg another squeeze to quiet him. I'm rapt.

The host greets Chrys. They chat for a bit about her upcoming movie, and she teases the details. It's a big one, with a five-time Oscar-nominated director to the name, and yet Chrys remains humble about the project. She chats animatedly, excited, as though she were merely a fan and not acting in the movie.

The crowd clearly loves her. They laugh at her jokes and clap at her accomplishments.

Naturally, the conversation steers toward *the* scandal. Her brief engagement to the one-and-only Eric North.

"What was the call like?" the host asks.

Chrys rests her hands in her lap. "Well, they asked me to play the part, and I was like—hmm, I could go to Paris, or I can spend the weekend crying in my Cheerios. Again."

A laugh from the audience.

"Our girl is good," I tell Eric.

"Very," he replies.

"I'm *dying* to know," the host continues dramatically. "What was it like being engaged to Eric North?"

Chrys cocks her head as though she's thinking. "He's a great friend but a *bad* fiancé. Are you familiar with the term *alpha-hole*?"

"Oh, *dish*."

"Well, he's an *incredibly* sore loser. I can't help it if I'm a crossword champion!"

Another laugh from the audience.

Eric frowns. "Turn it off."

"You *are* a sore loser," I counter. "She's not lying." He grunts. I steal the remote from him to turn the volume even higher.

The interviewer asks, "So tell us—does this mean Chrys Hudson is back on the market now? Or do you already have someone?"

Chrys bites her lip and smiles coyly. "Come on, David. Can't a girl keep *some* secrets?"

As if on cue, there's a knock on the door.

Eric and I exchange a quick glance.

"I'll get it," Eric says. He nearly launches out of the bed.

I can't help but smile. He's as eager as a kid at Christmas.

"Save some for me," I tell him, but he's already fastened the belt around his robe and exited the bedroom.

I can't blame him. My heart, too, races in my chest.

It's been far too long.

But now…
Our girl is home.

40

ERIC

I fling open the door. Chrys stands there with a smile and a bottle of champagne.

I'm not ashamed to say my heart skips a beat.

"You're a sight for sore eyes," I tell her.

"If your eyes are sore, you should get that checked, old man." She tilts her head toward the door. "Permission to come aboard?"

I flatten my palm against the doorframe, blocking her entrance with my arm. If she's going to be a brat, she's going to have to work for it. "Password."

She hugs the bottle of champagne to her chest and smiles sweetly. "Pretty please, Daddy."

That'll do. I raise my arm, and she ducks under the bridge.

Once Chrys is inside, I close the door behind her. Chrys makes herself at home—as she should. She is home when she's here. It's something of an unspoken pattern the three of us have agreed on. When Chrys isn't filming, or doing PR, or doing whatever million and one tasks we actors have to juggle, she ends up here. In our house. In our bed.

She sets the bottle on the kitchen counter and starts to unwrap the foil

"I like the outfit," she says. She glances at me, her eyes sweeping over my robe. "Were you two getting cozy without me?"

I step in beside her and cross my arms. "We were just watching your interview. *The Night Show*."

She abandons the bottle, foil half-ripped, and turns her complete attention toward me. "What'd you think?"

"According to you, I'm the biggest asshole in the world."

"Well." She brushes her thumb over my beard. "You kind of are. Besides. You should be thanking me."

"*Thanking* you? For what?"

"It adds to your mystique."

"Don't make me spank you."

She smiles. "Don't make me beg for it."

I flip her around and give her a quick, hard slap on the ass. She gasps and moans, assuming position. Her hands grip the edge of the kitchen counter, and she leans forward, just enough. Ready to take it again.

I push her short, black dress up over the roundness of her ass, baring the soft, white panties underneath. I spank her a second time. Hard. It's going to leave a welt, I know it.

She mewls softly.

There's a sigh. I glance up.

Nico steps into the room. "At least wait until we've opened the *champagne*," he complains, gesturing to the counter. "Animals."

Chrys pops up and rushes over to him. She nestles against him, and they hug and share a small kiss.

"Hello, dearest," he tells her, still cradling her in his arms.

"Hi." She smiles, blissful.

The sight of them together makes my heart pound.

Nico's not wrong. I *am* fucking feral.

162

"You shouldn't have brought the champagne," he says. "We're celebrating *you*."

"Hush and open it."

I take charge of the champagne. I pull down flutes from the drawers, chuck the foil off the top, and unwind the cage.

Out of the corner of my eye, I watch Nico play with Chrys' hair.

"We've missed you," Nico tells her.

"I missed you too," Chrys says. "I've been going crazy without you two. These past couple weeks have had me a little...well..."

"Pent-up?" Nico finishes.

The cork pops off. Loudly.

"Shit." I hold it at arm's length. Bubbles spill over, making a mess. I catch it at an angle and swallow back as much as I can.

"If you're going to spill half the bottle..." Nico cocks his head. "You may as well bring it in here."

I close the gap between us. Nico immediately arches up to meet my lips, but I put my hand on his chest, putting him in his place. I'm in my element now. In control.

Nico licks his lips.

"Do you want champagne?" I ask.

"Yes..."

"Yes, *what?*"

"Yes, please, Sir."

"Open your mouth."

He does. I put the bottle to my lips, feel the champagne fizzle in my mouth, and hold it.

When I kiss him, I slide my tongue against his, and I let it spill. It trickles down between our lips, messy. He swallows back as much as he can.

I turn to Chrys. "Would you like some as well?"

She bats her beautiful eyelashes. "Please, Daddy."

I take another swig from the bottle.

Fuck the flutes. We're animals.

I press my lips to hers. We kiss, and when I open my mouth, her tongue flicks inside, greedy. She sucks the champagne down and sighs when our lips part.

"Delicious," she murmurs.

"Yes. You are." She has that hazy, sex-hungry look in her eyes. So does Nico. I want to kiss the both of them until their lips bruise. Instead, I set the bottle down on the kitchen island and move my hands to her dress. "You're also wearing too many clothes."

Chrys makes it easy for me. She turns around and pulls her hair back over her shoulder so I can access the zipper on her back. I peel it down and kiss the soft skin as it's revealed —the back of her neck, her shoulder, her spine.

She shivers at my lips. I push her dress all the way down, and when I rise, I unclasp her bra as well. She shrugs out of both.

When she turns to face me now, she's wearing nothing but her panties...and a necklace. I hook the thin chain in my finger. It was hidden under her dress, but I can see it clearly now. Dipping between the round curves of her breasts sits her engagement ring, the ruby-red stone sparkling. It's the ring Nico picked out and the ring I gave her.

It awakens something in me to see her wearing it again. There's a heat in my blood, rising.

"I like this," I tell her.

Her smile is almost shy. She twists the ring between her fingers. "Me too. It makes me feel like you two are with me... even when you're not."

She's so fucking sweet, I want to pound her cunt until she screams.

The three of us kiss and touch and nibble at each other as we exit the living room and move toward the bedroom. Our robes and remaining clothes scatter across the hallway.

Chrys' panties go flying and end up on a horned mask hanging on the wall.

"Wait," Chrys says, putting her hand to Nico's chest. All three of us pause at the word. She tilts her head toward the glass sliding doors and asks, "What's the verdict on skinny-dipping?"

The hedges are thick and designed to keep prying eyes out. The backyard is our own private slice of paradise. I flick on the lights from inside the house, and the yard lights up. We have looping string lights across the foliage, plus low, yellow bulbs built into the stone on each side of the pool. There are lights in the pool as well, which make the water sparkle and glow.

It's a beautiful LA night. Clear. The stars are out, sprinkled in the sky.

Chrys is the first in. She doesn't hesitate; she just jumps straight in with a splash. Nico grabs the champagne, and the three of us sip straight from the bottle as we float around the pool. The water is still warm from the summer sun. It feels exquisite.

I kiss Chrys. Chrys kisses Nico. Nico kisses me. We take turns kissing and fondling and trading champagne from one mouth to the other. We're sloppy and decadent, and I can't get enough of the two of them.

Nico takes the bottle, and Chrys wraps her legs around my hips. I hold her up against me. She's completely weightless in the water, and her breasts press against my chest.

She's nothing but softness and sweetness. I hold her close, run my tongue over her throat, and nibble her ear.

I whisper here: "I want you."

41

CHRYS

*T*he night is hot. The pool is warm.

But Eric's confession makes me shudder.

I'm buoyant in his arms. I wrap my legs around his hips to keep from floating up. His erection nuzzles against my belly, hard and needy.

His tongue pries my mouth open, demanding and possessive. I sigh into his kiss. Behind me, I feel a second pair of hands dive into my hair, a second pair of lips kissing my throat, my shoulder.

All my life, I've been looking for a safe space.

And now, I've found it. Wedged between these two men who adore me.

Eric breaks the kiss and glides us through the water until I'm up against the wall. He pats the wall and says, "Puppy. Hop up."

Nico obeys. He slips out of the water and hangs his legs over the edge of the pool. He's dripping, and the moonlight glistens off his shoulders and back.

Eric reaches upward to hook his arm around the back of Nico's neck. He draws the other man down and into a rough kiss. I love the way they are together—the boundless love that exists between them.

Nico's eyes close blissfully as Eric releases him and moves his attention to his lover's body. He slips a hand up Nico's thigh and wraps his fingers around Nico's cock. Nico sighs, swelling to his full, impressive length until Eric pumps.

I unwind from Eric's lap. I want to make Nico whimper too. I lean in and press my lips to the tip of his cock.

"Oh, God," Nico says, his voice shuddering.

Eric's hand works Nico's base as I tease him with my tongue, tasting the chlorine from the pool and Nico's familiar, salty arousal.

His skin is velvet soft and hot between my lips, and it makes my body burn. When Eric reaches between my legs with his other hand to pet my pussy, his touch sends every nerve on fire. I gasp and rut my hips back against his hand, aching for the friction.

"You drive me crazy," Eric growls in my ear.

I can't help but grin. "I like you a little mad."

"Brat." He removes his hand from me, and now I feel the head of his cock between my legs. He's teasing my entrance, and I bite back a whimper. "Use your nice words."

I gasp. "Please, Daddy..."

The magic words. He pushes inside of me. I feel him stretch me, fill me. It's a delicious ache. I have one hand on the edge of the pool, the other on Nico's thigh, and I grip both for stability.

He's not wrong. He is wild for me.

His body is hard and strong behind me. I'm pressed against the slippery tiles as Eric thrusts hard against me. He sends bursts of pleasure through me, hitting my deepest places.

My legs go weak, and my knees buckle. I drop forward into Nico's lap. I'm buzzing with pleasure, with want, and I find myself pressing frantic kisses to his erection.

"Good girl," Nico praises, his voice honey smooth. He runs his fingers through my wet hair, and I swallow him down completely.

42

NICO

*T*his is close to heaven.

Water sloshes against the pool wall in time with Chrys' soft whimpers.

Her lips pull me toward ecstasy. The warmth of her mouth is unbearably sweet.

I love the way she gives herself so completely to us. I love her openness. I love the low grunts that come from Eric as he ruts against her. I love the electricity between the three of us that seems brighter than even the stars above.

I love, I love, *I love*.

"I love you," I blurt out, because the feeling is so intense, it feels like I'll explode if I can't get the words out. "I love you, I love you...*les amos*."

And then I do explode. Heart racing, lungs tight, my pleasure is pulled taut like the strings of a violin. Then it snaps. My breath catches, and I grip a handful of Chrys' hair as I burst, my orgasm spilling into her lips, down her throat.

Chrys makes a satisfied noise, almost like a purr. She swallows me down, and as she does, I feel her fingers grip my thigh tighter, her nails digging in.

She whines, drops me from her lips, and gets out the words, "Oh, fuck..."

Her eyebrows knit, and she cries out, shaking with her orgasm. She bows forward, her face burrowed against my leg, and I pet her hair, coaxing her through her release. Eric, too, gives a low-throated groan that I'm oh so familiar with, and the three of us pant and slide together, spent.

"I love you too," Chrys murmurs suddenly. "Both of you."

The metal from the ring around her neck is cool against my leg.

"I love you," Eric says. He touches her, pressing a kiss to her shoulder, but his deep blue eyes lock on mine, and I know he means both of us.

I could live in this moment forever, my body wonderfully sore, my heart cramped in my chest, too big and too full of love.

Maybe one day the world will be ready for the likes of us. Until then...

She's our little secret.

THE END

* * *

Note from Adora: Thank you for reading Mr. Hollywood's Secret! I hope you had as much fun with Eric, Nico, and Chrys as I did :)

If you enjoyed it, please consider leaving a review. Authors are like Tinkerbells, and applause keeps us going!

If you're hungry for more steamy MMF romance, you can join my newsletter to get the latest releases, and an exclusive free story!

Click here to join: https://adoracrooksbooks.com/gift/

Thanks again for reading! Keep reading for a peak into one of my MMF romances, "Truth or Dare."

XOXO,

Adora

TRUTH OR DARE

1

KENZI

*H*e's the most beautiful boy I've ever seen.

Raven-black hair cut short around his ears. Sky-blue eyes underneath dark, pensive eyebrows. Lips that are just a little too big for his face. Dimples when he smiles.

He sticks out from the pack—but how could he not?—well over six feet tall and towering over everyone. His body is all lean muscle, and he shows it off under the summer sun, wearing nothing but black boardshorts. He's sitting on the deck of a fishing boat, perched on the rim, like it's a throne, surrounded by a cawing group of three boys and two girls, all in swimsuit attire and drinking wine coolers and shitty beer. They're blasting some Top 40, and it's echoing up and down the sleepy dock of Hannsett Island Marina.

At eighteen, he's been dropped into the body of a god, and it's clear from his posse and his confident grin that he's decided to wield his newfound power by the way of Dionysus—chaos, destruction, and *boys will be boys*.

And I'm bored enough to be entranced by his peacocking.

The only thing I'm working on is a tan, playing through my new Gwen Stefani album, and a rereading of *Little Women* (don't we all want to be Jo?).

I'm lying on a towel, Walkman by my side, sprawled out on the top of Four's sailboat, *Sweet Serenity*, which is currently tied up in a slip directly across from the party boat.

Four and Pearl are downstairs (or "below deck" as Four likes to correct me), and every now and then I can hear the blender roar as they down margaritas.

"Four" is short for "stepdad number four."

Which is all he will be, until stepdad number five.

It's not that I have anything against him—he taught me blackjack and he smokes Cuban cigars and he wears his hair in a long gray ponytail which he somehow pulls off. It's just that he's temporary, and there's no point in getting attached to something that won't be around for very long, anyway.

He owns both a beach house and a sailboat at Hannsett Island, an island off Long Island that you have to take a ferry in order to get to, which means that Pearl and I are basically stranded here for the summer. Pearl is my mom, but I haven't called her "mom" since I was five. I have a very vivid memory of her breaking me of the habit in Gabriel's Butchery on the Upper West Side, after I'd ruined her effort to pick up a man in a black tweed turtleneck along with her black-pepper ground salami. Apparently, it's hard to flirt when you have a little rug rat tugging on your dress begging for attention.

Getting out of the stink and hot asphalt of a New York City summer seemed like a great idea at the time. Until I realized that Pearl and Four were going to be the ones drinking and necking...while I got stuck with no friends, limited internet access, and skin that burns before it tans.

It would be better if I wasn't here. I get that. This is Pearl and Four's romantic getaway. I'm the annoying teenager who gets pissy when she's gone more than twenty-four hours without her Myspace account.

My captivity is made only marginally better by the eye candy in slip 12A. I glance over the top of my book. Raven-Hair has got his legs splayed out, leaning back on his elbows, a posture that says *I own this room and everyone in it.* His friends address him as "King," and I can't tell yet if that's his name or if that's just his Holier Than Thou title.

God save us from the cockiness of a teenage boy.

I don't usually go gaga for jocks—they're too often assholes to girls like me, who got curvier once puberty hit. But there's something about his swagger that goes right between my legs. Maybe they grow boys differently in Long Island. Something in the water?

Or maybe it's just me. Nearly eighteen, never been kissed, hormones rocketing through me, making me boy-crazy, making me more of an *Amy* than a *Jo.*

King's boat is a tall motorboat with the words *Healing Touch* scrawled in gold cursive along the back. The engine is going now, gurgling, and it looks like they're getting ready to set off, even though I don't see any adults on board. Are they even old enough to drive that thing? And aren't they all at least semi-buzzed?

The water, I've learned, is lawless.

Curious, I move a headphone off my ear so I can snoop.

The dock boy unhooks the boat from the dock, untangling the lines and tossing them into the boat. Two more boys (obviously part of the party crew) come down the dock with a cooler between them.

"Get over here!" one of the girls shouts from the boat. "Or we'll leave you!"

I watch as the boys comically scramble over the side of the boat, carting the goods over first before tumbling in. Just as the final jock makes his landing, he puts his hand on the dock boy's chest. "Thanks, Dick Boy," I hear him sneer before giving the kid a shove. He goes tumbling backward and hits the water—much to the delight of everyone on board, who breaks into laughter.

Oh, *hell* no. I leap to my feet and throw a single barbed insult: "Assholes!"

177

It lands straight between the eyes of King, who—*now*—suddenly notices me. His eyes meet mine. They're way, way too blue to be real. His gaze feels like a bolt of lightning striking down my spine. It's hitting 90 degrees right now, yet my nipples are knots.

He gives me a cocky half-grin and shrugs a single shoulder as if to say, *Whoops.*

I feel the heat rise up my neck. Jerk.

The *Healing Touch* glugs as it leaves the slip, and every teenager on board hoots and hollers as they go further out to sea. I hope a kraken swallows them whole, honestly.

I leave my Walkman and book behind and leap from the edge of the sailboat to the wooden dock. The sun-charred slabs are stingingly hot underneath my bare feet, but I ignore the pain and crouch down to the edge to extend my hand.

"Need a hand?" I ask as the dock boy swims to the edge of the dock.

"I've got it," he grumbles, but as he scrabbles at the edge to get his footing, it's clear he *doesn't* have it. He takes my arm, and together we pull him up. His uniform—a white polo shirt with a small lighthouse stitched into the chest pocket and khaki pants—is soaked through. I pick a piece of seaweed from his shoulder, and he grimaces about it.

"Those guys are a bag of dicks," I tell him.

"Yeah," he says. "You don't know the half of it."

"Can I get you anything? A towel?"

"I'll live. The clothes aren't the problem." He's got these soft chestnut irises, and they meet my gaze for the first time. "You want to know the real tragedy?"

"Always."

He reaches into his pocket and pulls out a neatly rolled joint, now soaked and limp.

"RIP," he says.

I hold up a finger. "Hold on."

Why, yes. I have tricks up my sleeve. I reach into my

bikini, where I've stashed away my one vice from Four and Pearl: a rolled joint and a lighter. For the moments I really need to escape.

For the first time, Dock Boy smiles. "Hello, new best friend."

"You can call me Kenzi."

*　*　*

Dock Boy's real name is Donovan. His real age is nineteen. I haven't discovered his real hair color yet, but I know it's not black because he keeps having to towel off his neck when the dark hair dye drips down around his ears.

Hannsett Island Marina is a self-contained ecosystem, complete with its own restaurant (the Blue Heron, accessible by the public) and a slew of private facilities: a general store, a private pool, a communal shower/restroom/locker room, and a laundry room.

There are only two sets of washers and dryers in the laundry room. Donovan sits on one of the washers, I sit on the fold-out table, and we pass my joint back and forth as his clothes tumble dry.

He's wearing only his boxers, but they look enough like a bathing suit that it's somehow not obscene. Doesn't keep me from admiring his body, though. He's lean, not quite stacked like the jocks, but I like the softness of him. He's kept on this thick leather-woven bracelet and a simple chain necklace with a ring on it.

"Promise ring?" I ask and point to it.

He frowns at that. "My mom's wedding ring."

"Divorced?"

"Deceased."

"I'm sorry."

He shrugs, and that's the end of that conversation.

I get it. I have things that *were* my dad's, sort of. Pearl kept

179

his record player and a few tattered albums. I play them sometimes, but only because I like music, not because I liked him. He died when I was just a kid, and the memories I have aren't great ones, so we never had the kind of connection that inspired me to carry around any of his trinkets.

My head is a little hazy, and I swish my legs under the table. I feel small, but not in a bad way. The comfort of careless innocence. "So why do those guys hate you?"

Donovan thins his lips. He taps ash off onto the quarter slot. "I'm a loser. I'm gay. I don't have a yacht or a summer house. Take your pick."

"That's fucked-up. Have you told anyone about it?"

Donovan's eyes sharpen. "*Who?* No one cares. Jason King and his crew of idiots basically run this island."

King. That clicks. "Jason King...is that the tall one?"

"Tall, blue-eyed, and beautiful? That's the one. He's a rare breed of island native. Have you visited the Lighthouse Medical Center yet?"

"Nope, and from the sound of it, I don't want to."

"Good call. It's Hannsett Island's pride and joy, though. And the island's cash cow. Jason's dad owns it, which basically makes him richer than God. They have a mansion in the Dunes. Two boats. And a second house Upstate."

"All hail the Kings," I say which draws a little wry smile from Donovan. He holds out the joint in offering, but I shake my head. I'm already floating. An ant crawls over my knuckles, its tiny legs tickling, and I let it. I watch its perilous odyssey across the back of my hand and then back onto the table.

"Why are the pretty ones always jerks?" I wonder out loud.

I can feel Donovan looking at me. "You don't seem jerkish."

I stick my tongue out at him. He laughs.

2

DONOVAN

enzi quickly becomes my favorite part of my day.

Which isn't hard, when my days mostly involve casting off, casting on, buffing the deck, polishing sideboards, rinse, repeat.

I grind polish over fifty-foot yachts until I'm caked in sweat and my fists refuse to unclench. I can usually find Kenzi at the pool or sunbathing on her stepdad's boat, *Sweet Serenity*. She's easy to steal away for a smoke break, or a dip in the pool, or just a chat over watermelon slices and H2O.

Kenzi loves music, above all, and some days we just take turns listening to her Walkman. Eventually, she opens up her notebook and shows me some of the lyrics she's working on. She wants to be a songwriter. Not a singer/songwriter—just a songwriter. Her lyrics are good. Really good. I call her the female Bernie Taupin. She smiles when I say that.

Plus, King's crew tends me leave me alone when I'm with her. So. That's a silver lining.

We talk about our plans for next year—or lack thereof. She's on the waitlist for Berklee College and hasn't heard back, so as far as she's concerned, she's taking a gap year. I can relate—I've been in limbo for the past year as Dad and I try our luck with scholarship lotto. So far, no hits.

Except for Tomorrow's Doctors.

Every summer, the Lighthouse Medical Center runs a four-week program for what they call "Tomorrow's Doctors." Ages 17-19. Throw the minnows in the pond. See if they can swim.

So, after work, I clock out, hop on my bike, and pedal as fast as I can out of the marina, up the road that winds alongside the dunes, all the way to the medical center.

The first thing you see when you approach the medical center is the lighthouse itself. The lighthouse hasn't been in operation for over fifty years, but it's still a beautiful thing. Red brick, restored to its former glory, with a black chrome dome. The light doesn't shine anymore, except for special occasions—holiday light shows, that sort of thing.

The lighthouse is flanked by three buildings: the pediatric wing, the general care and rehabilitation wing, and the emergency wing. I'm hit with the smell of freshly cut grass as I cut across the large lawn to park my bike on the rack. I don't lock my bike here; there's no need. Everyone on the island stays on the island.

I've got my knapsack stuffed in a milk carton my dad looped to the back of my bike for storage, and I quickly throw it on my shoulders before heading inside.

Entering the Lighthouse Medical Center doesn't knock the breath out of me like it used to. But the first couple of times, yeah, it was hard not to be impressed. The lobby sits underneath a domed ceiling, all glass. Through it, you can see the top of the lighthouse.

As soon as the doors open, you come face-to-face with a giant art deco–style sculpture of a man on one knee. He has his hand open, the sun sitting in the palm of his hand. Underneath the sculpture, the words run in a band: "A Guiding Light Through the Dark."

The only thing more impressive than the talented, skilled doctors at Lighthouse Medical Center are the deep pockets of the donors.

It's the kind of money a guy like me can't even begin to wrap my head around.

I grip the straps of my backpack a little tighter and trudge ahead.

Tomorrow's Doctors meet on the second level of the rehab wing, which is otherwise blocked off for professionals. It's mostly storage here—a lot of doors marked "Keep Out." Labs with expensive equipment. I walk down the hall, to the doctors' mess. There's a kitchenette here, complete with a coffee machine, a small fridge, and a snack machine. In the adjoining room are bunk beds for the on-call doctors who pull long hours. The lockers that line the room are meant for the staff, but Tomorrow's Doctors get six spots reserved at the far end.

I'm not the only one here. The cast are as follows:

Jason: the leader of the pack, his father's prodigy.

Nick: Jason's best friend, stocky, the kind of guy who will argue with you that his shirt is *salmon*, not pink.

Brett: a blond-haired jock, usually found strutting around with a volleyball.

They're loitering around the circular table. Nick has taken a bag of Doritos from the snack pile, and it makes his fingers orange.

"C'mon, Jason," Nick is whining. "Throw us a bone."

"A gentleman never tells," I hear Jason say.

"Since when are you a gentleman?" Brett protests. "Spill."

I go to my own locker, pop it open, and start to shove my things in it.

"I *can* tell you one thing," Jason gives in.

"What?"

"Her sister was better."

Gross. His friends howl with laughter, but I have a hard

time hiding my disdain. My locker rattles when I slam it, and I hear their laughter come to a halt.

"Hey, Nick," Jason says, "does something smell fishy to you?"

"Yeah," Nick says, "smells like the whole fresh market just walked in."

My jaw clenches. I keep my eyes on the floor, keep my back to them, and ignore their obnoxious cackles as I enter the adjoining room.

We take our class sessions in a repurposed conference room, with a long oval table surrounded by black swivel chairs. The other two students have already taken their seats, notebooks open. I wouldn't call them friends. No one is exactly *friendly* to me, since King and his clan put a target on my back last summer and therefore fraternizing with me is social suicide.

It wasn't always like this. Believe or not, Jason and I used to be almost-friends. Between the beachgoers and the patients in and out of the clinic, Hannsett is an island of transplants. No one stays here very long.

Except for me and Jason. We're a rarity. Year-around natives. Hannsett Island is like a prison—you love the one you're with. Before he surrounded himself with summer partygoers who call him *King* and decided he preferred obnoxious boat parties, frat boys, and picking on anyone he considered an easy target.

Which included me.

I sit next to Ernest, who is quiet and generally ignores me, which I'll take over taunting. Even he rolls his chair a little further away from me today, though.

I did spend half of the day cleaning a fishing boat. Maybe I do smell like chum.

Eventually, Jason's crew takes their seats, and our teacher arrives. Dr. Esmeralda is a middle-aged Black woman who has been at the hospital as long as I have. She was here when my mom got sick, so I feel like I already know her. She has a warm bedside manner, but she's stoic in the classroom.

"Let's see who did the precursory reading," she says once we're all settled in. "Three patients enter the emergency room with heat-related illnesses—something we get a lot of at Hannsett. The first patient is seventy-two, has fainted, and feels dizzy. The second patient is a homeless man, who seems confused and exhibits poor coordination; he also has hot, dry skin. The third is a swimmer with tachycardia and nausea. Who do you see first?"

Her eyes scan the room. Then they land on— "Jason."

Jason lifts his head from his notebook. He blinks as though he's come out of a dream. "Um…"

"*Um?* That isn't a diagnosis I've ever heard of."

A ripple of laughter across the room. Jason isn't laughing, though. He has the look of a bull post-matador fight. Wounded. Tired. And plotting to run everyone through with his horns as soon as he gets his strength back.

"Can you repeat the question?" he asks.

"No." Dr. Esmerelda's gaze swings over to me. "Donovan."

"I'd treat the homeless patient first," I recite immediately. "The temperature of his skin suggests heat stroke, which can be life threatening for someone in his condition."

"Seems you have a guardian angel, Jason," Dr. Esmerelda says. "Donovan just resurrected your patient. Let's spend less time hitting the beach this summer and more time hitting the books."

I can feel Jason's stare, like ice chips sliding down my spine.

I ignore it and press my pen deep into the paper, making a welt in my journal. I'm going to pay for opening my big dumb mouth later, but…

At least my hypothetical patient lived.

* * *

I make a beeline to my locker after class. Jason and his crew are loitering. Jason is sitting on the counter with his shoes on the table.

Respect is for lesser humans, apparently.

He looks at me, and there's a glint in his eyes I don't like.

"Sup, Angel?" he asks.

Angel. Jesus Christ. I guess I have Dr. Esmerelda to thank for my new nickname now.

I ignore him and go to my locker.

"Hey," Brett chimes in, "King is talking to you."

My jaw clenches. *Let's rip this Band-Aid.* "What?"

"What're you doing tonight? You wanna come out?"

"Out?" I repeat skeptically.

"Yeah. We're having a party tonight."

Is Jason...inviting me to a party? Seems unlikely. His impossibly tall frame is arched over, one leg crooked on a chair. He's panther-like and coy in his body language, his knees slightly splayed, his broad shoulders angled back. His tight pants do nothing to hide the package underneath, and I hate myself for noticing these details about him.

His body language always makes him look like he's flirting...even when he isn't.

His wolf's grin makes me suspicious.

"Good for you," I say.

"So you coming?"

I consider my options. I should say no. On the other hand. If this is a genuine invitation, a party might be fun. When was the last time I was invited to something like that—?

Never. The answer is never.

"Maybe," I say as I open my locker, "I'll have to check with—"

But as soon as the door swings open, two wet bodies fly out at me. Huge, slippery bass flip out of my locker and slap against my chest. The smell that my locker unleashes is atrocious.

Jason and his crew cackles. I feel Jason's hand slap on my shoulder. "You know what?" he says. "Maybe next time. Think you should go home and...shower this off." He steps backward out the door. Before he leaves, he has the audacity to wink. "Later, Angel."

The dead fish leak onto the ground. So much for sterilization.

Fucking dick.

* * *

Every muscle in my body hurts as I bike back to the marina.

Sunsets are beautiful at Hannsett Island. Pink and lavender streaks across the sky and spills across the water. The boats sway softly, each tucked away safely in their slip. We have a pair of swans that nest in the tallgrass every year and they make small ripples in the glass-like water. Every now and then, a gull calls out or a mainline bangs against the mast, giving out a gong-like sound. Other than that, it's still. Quiet.

Paradise is nice—if you're rich enough to enjoy it. My dad and I live in a trailer. It's tucked away behind the pool. They don't let us park it in the parking lot, "too unsightly" for the boat owners. Instead, we're hidden behind the pine trees, in a strip of dirt where grass once was.

I roll my bike through the thicket and rest it against a tree. Dad is cooking up dinner on the BBQ, and the smell of burning meat makes my stomach pinch.

"Dinner's ready in five," Dad says.

Things dad never says:

How was your day?

Are those boys still taunting you?

Why do you smell like fish?

187

Why do you smell like pot?

Is everything okay?

Our conversations are mostly functional: can you do this? / this is done. Food is ready / pass the ketchup.

Which is fine. He's got skin like leather from being in the sun and looks twice as old as he should. He's as exhausted as I am. We don't have the time or energy for a heart-to-heart.

"Be right there," I say. I start inside the trailer. We have a jar we share, and I dump my tips in it. It's not much, but we'll stay fed for the rest of the week.

Our trailer has a sink in the front, a cushioned bench (my bed), a bathroom, and a main cabin in the back (Dad's bed). I stretch across the bench and lie down. Just for a second, I tell myself.

But as soon as my eyes close, I'm out.

I don't know how long I've slept, but I wake up to my father's hand on my shoulder. Rough hands, gentle squeeze. "Hey, kiddo," he murmurs. "Some girl is here to see you."

I blink awake, disoriented. My hair is a mess. I'm still in my sweat-stained uniform. I'm not fit for humans. A girl?

Only one girl it could be. I descend the steps and glance around.

Kenzi stands there. She's wearing a cute yellow dress with strappy shoulders. Her black hair is in swoopy waves. Green eyes shining like sea glass.

The sight of her makes me feel a weird way, a way I don't usually feel about girls. My heart launches itself against my chest like a wild animal suddenly uncaged.

"What's up?" I ask. Casual.

She half-grins, looking shy—my father usually has that effect on people; he's hard-edged and scary. But she holds up a paper plate, a piece of cake on it, and says, "I come bearing gifts."

She's a gift: pristine and pretty, fresh off the spotless deck of her stepdad's boat.

I'm filthy and burningly aware of the eyesore that is the trailer.

I sway on the balls of my feet, deliberating. "Give me one second."

I close the door on her and squeeze past my dad. "You want me to tell her to go?" he asks.

"No." I'm tearing off my clothes, ripping a paper towel off, dampening it, and wetting my face, the back of my neck, all the parts of me that feel grimy. I pull on black jeans, a black shirt. Run my fingers through my hair. I slip my lip ring into my bottom lip—I have to take it out while I work (Mr. King's orders), but I try to pop it in once I'm off to keep the hole from closing up.

"Your burger is still on the grill," Dad reminds me.

"Thanks. I'll grab it later."

I slip outside and close the door behind me. No more dock boy.

Kenzi is sitting on my stump. She glances up, and her eyes sweep over me. "So this is what Donovans look like in their natural habitat."

"Mmhm." There's a sugar flower on her slice of cake, and I swipe it between my fingers and pop it in my mouth. "Whose birthday is it?"

"Mine."

I squint at her. "Are you serious?"

"Lucky number eighteen."

"That's a big one."

"So I've been told." If she's put off by the trailer, BBQ pit, or my growly father, she doesn't show it. The opposite, actually; she looks right at home.

"Wanna take a walk?" I ask her.

"Sure."

She hands over the plate and a plastic fork, and we walk through the grass and behind the fenced-in pool.

The crickets sing. Fireflies blink. We find a large slab of

stone to sit on. We watch an egret wade her long legs through the tall grass at the edge of the water.

All of this nighttime peace is interrupted only by the true wildlife of Hannsett Island: the *Healing Touch* is booming tonight, blaring loud pop music.

Jason King and his merry band of popular kids never quit.

"Wanna play a game?" Kenzi asks as we pick at the cake.

"Sure."

"Truth or dare?"

"Dare."

"I dare you to catch a firefly."

"Hold this." I hand her the plate, and she takes it. I get up and move just a little ways into the long cattail bushes. There's a bunch of small lights, blinking on and off. Fireflies are pretty, but dumb and slow. I cup one in both my hands, then come back over to Kenzi.

"Check it out." I open my hands, just a little. She leans over, her head nearly bumping mine. Inside my curved fingers, the trapped firefly glows, illuminating my palms.

"Nice," Kenzi murmurs. Her breath warms my hands.

"You want to glow?" I ask her.

She narrows her eyes at me. "What, like rip his butt off and rub it on our faces?"

"Well—"

"Psychopath. Let it go."

"Your lucky day, little guy," I tell him. I open my hands, and the firefly flies out, waving drunkenly through the sky.

"Your turn," I tell Kenzi as we sit back down on the stone. "Truth or dare?"

"Truth," she says, which I think is brave.

"What's the one thing you want to do now that you're eighteen?"

She lets out a small laugh and rubs the back of her neck. "Honestly?"

"That's why it's called *truth*."

"Okay. I want to lose my virginity." She shrugs. "I know that's like...pedestrian."

"It's not."

"And I know it's a *big deal* for some people. But I don't know...I just sort of want to rip off the Band-Aid. You know?"

"Quick and fast?"

"Okay, maybe not *that* much like ripping off a Band-Aid. But just...simple. No complications. With someone I trust, ideally. And then it'll be over with, and I can go about my life without this *thing* hanging over my head." Her emerald eyes blink at me. "Do you think I'm cold?"

"No," I tell her. "It's your body. You should do whatever you want with it."

She points her fork at me. "Thank you. You *get* me."

And I get it: I'm her gay best friend who she can open up to about things like this. Her blossoming sexuality. Her slutty summer plans. I am a man she can talk to fearlessly, without worrying that I'll turn around and try to kiss her.

So why is this conversation making me hard?

"Okay, you now," she says.

"What about me?"

"Truth or dare, Donovan?"

As if truth is even an option right now. "Dare."

She nods toward the party boat. "I dare you to give them a taste of their own medicine."

An idea forms. I put down the paper plate and stand up. "Only if you come with me."

"Obviously, I'm in." I reach out a hand, and she takes it. Her hand feels so soft in mine.

* * *

I lead Kenzi down the dock.

It's illuminated by dock lights, these big, bulky things that

191

are swamped by moths. We walk slowly down the wooden panels so they don't creak too loudly.

It turns out to be overkill. By time we get to the *Healing Touch*, we don't see anyone on the back—they've moved the party to the bow of the boat. We can hear beer cans cracking, music blaring, and rancorous laughter, but we can't see them...

And more importantly, they can't see us.

I point to the cleats, which keep the boat tied up to the dock. "You get the ones on the other side," I whisper to Kenzi. "I'll take these."

She sneaks around the side of the boat. I crouch down on the edge of the dock and unwind the thick rope from the cleats. As quietly as I can, I toss the rope onto the deck of the boat.

Kenzi comes back around, crouching behind the lights. "Done!"

I put my palms on the side of the boat. "On the count of three...push."

I count, and together, we give the boat a hefty push. It doesn't take much. It's a still night, and soundlessly, slowly, the boat follows the momentum of our push and drifts out of the slip and into the inky black water.

In the enclosed marina...it's not going far. But it's going to give them a hell of a shock when they realize what's going on.

Which happens sooner than I think.

"Whoa, are we moving, or is it just me?" a female voice hiccups from the bow.

"Run!" I whisper urgently to Kenzi.

We race down the dock, up the bridge, and behind the tall cattails by the pool. The tall grass tickles our ankles. We collide together, and I hook my arm around her to slow her down. "Look," I tell her.

Between the cattail reeds, we can see the chaos below.

The *Healing Touch* floats around aimlessly and lists toward one of the yachts. There are shouts from the jocks, then shouts from the people on the yacht, and they take out long poles in attempt to push the *Healing Touch* away before the two boats bump. The *Healing Touch* starts drifting away from the yacht then…and straight into a mudbank.

I can feel Kenzi's warm breath on my neck. Her heart is beating so fast I can feel it, tiny thumps against my bare arm. "Oh my God…" she says. "I'm sorry if you get in trouble for that."

"You kidding?" I tell her. "This is the best night of my life."

I could kiss her right now.

It's an urge, tugging on me, my heart strung like a marionette.

I could kiss her. We're so close like this. Her eyes meet mine, and for a second, I think she's thinking the same thing.

And then a splash catches our attention. We look back to the boat. Jason and Nick are in the mud now, water up to their waists, trying to push the boat back out. The boat makes a terrible grinding noise as someone tries to start up the engine. Jason King's swears can be heard all throughout the marina.

Kenzi puts her hand on her mouth and laughs.

The moment is gone, but we don't break apart.

We stay like this, locked together, watching the well-earned comedy play out below.

3

JASON

*Y*ou've caught me.

I'm an asshole. A Grade A bully. A jerk in sheep's clothing.

Meanness is a pin stuck between my shoulder blades, and I can't reach to get it out.

I swim until I can't feel the pin anymore. Until I can't feel anything but searing heat in my arms. Cramps in my legs. Lungs that feel like they're going to burst.

Finally, I pull myself back onto shore. Salt and sand cling to me.

It's a beautiful goddamn day on Hannsett Island. Like every summer day.

Bayside Beach is packed. Families under huge, multicolored umbrellas. People playing Frisbee. Volleyball. Seagulls fighting over french fries.

Amy lies sprawled across a beach towel, *Cosmo* magazine in her lap. She's wearing a bikini that barely covers her and a hat so big, it's essentially a second umbrella. When I step over her to grab a towel from the bag, she screams, "You're dripping on me!"

"Bet that's not the first time," Nick snickers. Nick sits in the fold-out beach chair, a dollop of sunscreen smeared down his nose, and Amy throws her magazine at him.

I pop open the cooler, but there's nothing but beers in here. "We have any water?"

Nick looks at Amy, who shrugs. I rummage around until I find a hard seltzer. Close enough. I chug that instead as I towel off water from the back of my neck.

"Hey," Nick says, "tell King what you told me."

Amy holds on to her hat and points across the beach. "That's the girl."

My eyes follow her finger. I recognize the girl in question immediately as the newbie from across the dock. She's sitting with her mother and one of my dad's friends—Terry. She's wearing a red one-piece and has headphones on. Big sunglasses on. She's sprawled across the towel, arm draped over her eyes. Blocking out the world.

The sight of her on full display like that—vulnerable, open—it does something to me. I feel my heartbeat pick up, only it's got nothing to do with my swim.

"What about her?" I ask.

Amy looks up at me, lips curled, pleased with herself. "She's the one I saw with Dick Boy. They're like *besties* now or whatever. They took the ropes off your dad's boat and pushed it away."

So *she's* the source of all my trouble. Anger is a heat, not an emotion. It burns and doesn't let up. My pin digs a little deeper.

I clasp my hand over Nick's shoulder to get his attention.

"Get everyone together," I tell him. "Let's do a bonfire tonight."

"Hell yeah!"

"Hey." Amy pops up, her body brushing mine. She has sand stuck all up the back of her arms, and she tickles the tips of her fingers over my bare abdomen. "Wanna come get some ice cream with me?"

The look in her eyes tells me *ice cream* isn't the only thing she wants in her mouth.

But I'm wound too tight. Burning too hot.

"Later," I tell her. "I'm going back in."

I need to clear my head in a way that only salt water can cure. Extinguish this rage before it consumes me. I toss the beach towel back down and dive back into the water.

4

KENZI

*L*ive piano music plays. Candlelight flickers over white tablecloth.

Pearl has dressed me in white. Which is not a good look for me. I look like a cream puff, the dress bunching awkwardly over my tummy. I crush my crème brûlée with my fork.

The Blue Heron is the high-end restaurant that overlooks the marina. It has two entrances, one for the "common folk" of Long Island, and a second entrance exclusively for the boat owners. The restaurant overlooks the marina, and you can see boats swaying in their slips through the siding. The Blue Heron calls itself the best place to catch the sunset on all of Hannsett Island, and they're not wrong.

It's incredibly romantic. And incredibly *awkward* when you're sitting across from your mother and her new catch, who are both caught under the spell of the ambiance.

What is it about candlelight that makes people so disgustingly gooey?

"God, that sunset is beautiful," Pearl muses, touching her manicured nails to her lips.

Four peels her blonde hair from her shoulder and places a

kiss on the bare skin there. "The *second* most beautiful thing here," he muses.

She laughs, a high bell-like sound which is definitely not genuine. I make a vomiting noise.

"*Kenzi.*" Pearl says my name as a warning, her eyes slits.

I pout. I crack another layer of toasted caramel.

Out of the corner of my eye, I see him. Jason King. The temperature practically changes when the King family enters the restaurant.

They're royalty. Jason's father is a salt-and-pepper high-baller—perfectly groomed, wearing a blazer and a watch they could probably see from space. Mrs. King is ageless, tanned, and a Hollywood classic beauty. She's fiddling with the shirt collar of what must be Jason's older brother—they have the same strong jaw, same bright eyes, and the same prowling presence of a cougar.

Jason looks different without his beach boardshorts and his posse. His shirt is buttoned up all the way to his Adam's apple, and the collar looks tight. He's holding his wrist, hands falling about to his groin—classic defensive posture. He's the tallest one in his family, a full head taller than his father, but next to the other man, he's shrunken, somehow. His shoulders are hunched, head half-bowed like a chastised dog.

Jason might be the king of high schoolers, but in his father's shadow, he's a meager *prince*. And it shows.

Mr. King smiles past the concierge, and the owner of the Blue Heron greets him personally with a stiff handshake. I find my eyes following them—the King family has become my new favorite nature documentary. *And here, we see the Kings in the wild, prowling over their domain...*

Blue sapphire eyes meet mine. *Oh shit.* I've been caught staring. I look away just when Jason's penetrating gaze connects with mine. Where to put my eyes? Outside. On the pearly stars. I twist my hair in my fingers.

Out of the corner of my vision, a too-tall figure approaches. "Shit," I whisper under my breath.

"Mr. Blake. Missus P." Jason stands at the edge of our table, polite as a fucking church mouse.

"Jason." Four smiles. He rests his hand on the back of Pearl's neck. "How's it going, son? Is your family here?"

"Yes, sir." Jason's eyes fix on me again. "I'm sorry to interrupt your dinner. Can I have a word with Kenzi?"

I roll my eyes and pick a breadstick off the table. I chew it the way Bugs Bunny might nibble his carrot in front of Elmer—*you're not the boss of me.* "Whatever you have to say, you can say in front of the table," I tell him.

"Okay." His eyes are sparkling. There's that mischief again. He comes out with it: "You're the one who cast off my boat."

He doesn't look pissed. If anything, he looks...amused? There's that smug smirk climbing his lips.

I shrug. "Maybe. Maybe not."

"Wanna come to a bonfire tonight?"

"Oh, a bonfire, honey, that sounds like fun!" Pearl says too enthusiastically.

"*Pearl,*" I chastise her. She's completely ruining my cool.

Pearl sighs loudly. "Excuse me for wanting you to have some teenage escapades while you're still young."

Jason eyes me. "I'll drive."

I pretend to consider it. "Can I bring my friend?"

"Who's your friend?"

"Donovan."

A sliver of something cruel slides across Jason's blue eyes. "I don't think he'd like the crowd."

"By that, you mean you don't think the crowd would like him?"

His mouth sets. "Whichever."

I shrug. "Then it doesn't sound like my crowd, either."

I scoop a forkful of crème brûlée while Jason considers. "Okay," he says finally. "He can come."

"Cool. You can pick me up later."

Jason's smile returns. Calm. Controlled. Cocky. "See you then." Then he nods toward Four and Pearl. "Enjoy the rest of your dinner."

With that, he turns and leaves to join his own family again. They have, obviously, the best table in the house, with a perfect view of the boats swaying in the marina.

Pearl puts her lips to her wineglass. "He's cute," she says into her pinot noir and wiggles her eyebrows.

"If you're into...*that*." I shrug and try not to blush.

"What did he mean about his boat?" Four asks, his brow furrowed.

"Hey!" I jump in with a quick change of topic. "I was thinking—can you teach me how to fish tomorrow?"

5

DONOVAN

"*K*iddo."

My eyes pry themselves open. As the sleep clears, the Sundance Kid races across the screen, shouting for his partner in crime.

Our TV is a small, square box, which is propped up on the fold-out table in front of us, along with a few empty beers and scraps from dinner.

I've passed out in the crook of my dad's arm. And drooled on myself.

Real baller right here.

Dad points to the window. "Your secret admirer is back."

As if on cue, there's a *plink!* against the window. A muffled voice: "Donovan!"

I jump up and wipe my mouth with the back of my arm. I fling open the door of our trailer.

She's there, looking ethereal in a white dress and a dangerous smile.

I hang halfway out the door. "Hey."

"Hey," she says. Small pile of acorns in her hand. And then: "Wanna come to a party tonight?"

"Sounds gross."

"Which is why I'm inviting you, nimrod."

I stifle a grin. "Okay."

* * *

Jason picks us up in a golf cart. Which is not the ride we expected.

We both changed for the occasion—she's wearing a bathing suit underneath tiny shorts, a Hawaiian shirt, and bright orange sneakers and, somehow, pulls it all off. I'm in my one pair of pants without holes in them, a black button-up with the top buttons undone. Kenzi has also had her fun running a little gel through my hair and adding some liner to my eyes. I don't hate either of it.

Jason is classic prep boy chic, in his polo shirt, khaki pants.

"What, no hot rod?" Kenzi asks as she climbs into the back of the cart. I follow suit, gripping the side.

"It's the only thing my dad lets me drive after I wrecked the Buick." As he starts it back up, Jason adds, "And the Mercedes."

Hannsett Island is a little over five miles long, so it's golf cart–friendly.

Jason drives us to the beach on the east end. The sunset stretches ribbons of orange and pink across the sky and ocean. The air tastes dry and salty.

Hannsett Island has two main beaches: bayside and cliff-side. We're going to the cliffs now, which has choppier surf and therefore is less populated by tourists. The cliffs are made of clay, and after the rain, you can scoop your fingers through it and draw clay tattoos over your skin, like henna.

We can hear the party before we see it. Jason parks, we hop out, and he lifts a huge cooler that clinks when he carries it. Kenzi and I are in charge of the more manageable things— a couple of beach towels, a fold-out chair.

We climb the sand dune. The sun is dying, but we have plenty of light—a roaring bonfire in the middle of the beach. A boombox blares. Someone picks a guitar to an entirely different song. When Jason enters the scene, he's greeted with a war cry. He lifts his hand in acknowledgement. The King settling his buzzed and blazed clan.

This is not my clique—hell, this isn't even the same *species*. They are the rich and beautiful of Hannsett Island. I'm the guy who polishes Daddy's boat.

I feel my feet slow down, toes sinking in the sand the closer we get to the group.

Jason's core gang circles him. He points to me and Kenzi.

"This is Kenzi. Kenzi, this is Nick, Amy, and Brett."

Nick glares at me. "What's Dick Boy doing here?"

I brace for impact.

"I invited him," Jason says, which surprises me. He's claiming me. Then Jason's eyes sweep over Nick. "Go grab him a beer, yeah?"

They're bowing up—two stags with clashing horns. And then Nick breaks.

"Yeah," Nick says. "Okay."

Ah. So this is what it feels like to be blessed by the protection of Saint King himself.

Nick doesn't stop glaring at me, but he obeys, pulling two High Lifes out of the cooler. He hands one to me and one to Kenzi.

I take it and swallow back my small victory. I'm not used to the taste.

Amy—all thin limbs and blonde hair—leans her body into Jason's. She plays with the collar of his shirt. "Can I steal you for a second?"

"Sure," Jason grins. "Be right back."

He won't be *right* back, not if the hungry look in Amy's eyes is any indication as she drags him through the dune grass.

Kenzi plops down next to the guitarist. "So!" she says cheerfully, "Can you play anything other than Kumbaya?"

Kenzi is vivacious and bright. She might not fit the mold —Barbie-doll girls with big tits and empty heads—but she has a cutting wit and is "one of the boys". Maybe they can smell the entitlement on her, like a pheromone. They accept her into the group, and she blends in well.

Meanwhile, I sit beside her, quietly drink my beer, and sift sand between my toes. The lower layer still retains the day's heat.

Eventually, Kenzi and I peel off from the heat of the bonfire. We end up sitting on a dried-out husk of fallen tree, drinking and watching the sea creep up.

Kenzi points at the stars. "That's Big Bird."

"I think you mean Big Bear."

"No. Big Bird. Look at his beak!"

I laugh. The beers have made me hazy. "So I guess you're going to be an astronaut when you get older, huh?"

"I might." She turns to me. "What about you?"

"Doctor."

"Seriously?"

I nod. "It's all I've ever wanted to do. When my mom got sick…chemo and all that. The doctors that took care of her; they were my heroes. I want to do that for someone else."

"That's beautiful."

"Plus. The salary is nice."

"Ah, *there* it is."

We laugh. Out of the corner of my eye, I see Jason leave the bonfire to come join us.

He's lost his shirt, and it's hard to avoid looking at the glint of his muscled abdomen.

"Hey, beautifuls." Jason flops down beside us. He's got his back on the sand, and when he moves, I see it sticking to his shoulder blades.

"I think it's flirting with you, Kenzi," I tell her.

Jason cranes his neck back at us. "You having fun?"

"Not as much fun as you." Kenzi pokes his side with her toes. "You have lipstick on your neck, champ."

Jason rubs the side of his neck. "Is it my color?"

"A little bright."

"Hey," Jason says. "You guys wanna play a game?"

"What?"

"Spin the bottle?" Jason ventures.

"I'd rather give myself a lobotomy," I answer.

"Truth or dare?" Kenzi offers.

Jason snaps his fingers and points at her. "Bingo. Truth or dare, Kenzi?"

She grins. "Dare."

"Alright. I dare you to jump in the water."

Kenzi snorts a laugh. "Alright. Can do."

With that, she stands up and starts unbuttoning her shirt.

Kenzi is a lot of things. *Afraid* isn't one of them.

I grip the neck of my bottle a little tighter as I watch her fingers work off her buttons, one after the other. The firelight is licking at her skin, casting flickering shadows from the downward tilt of her chin, the curves of her breasts.

I remind my body to be still. I remind myself not to lick my lips like a hungry wolf. Everything in me goes rigid, though, when she drops her shirt and wiggles out of her pants.

I try to remind myself that I've seen her in a bathing suit before. But there's something about tonight. The way the bonfire light makes her creamy skin golden. The way her dark hair falls around her shoulders. That small dip in her back, inviting the touch of a hand.

I'm painfully hard. And I'm not alone. Jason watches her undress, his eyes never leaving her.

She glances back at us. Narrows her eyes. A light grin rests on her lips. "What's up? First time seeing a fat girl in a bikini?"

Then she flips us the bird and rushes to the water. There's a whoop from the firepit. She dives into the water, her pearly white body vanishing in the dark water.

For a second, all I can hear is the rushing of my own blood.

"So what's the deal with you two?" Jason asks suddenly.

I weigh the question. "What do you mean?"

"Friends? Dating? Friends with benefits?"

My laugh that escapes me is more like a hiss. My jaw won't unclench.

"Look—it's not any of my business if you're gay. Or bi. Or whatever. But there is something I want you to know." Jason puts his hand on the driftwood. The way we're positioned right now—me, splayed out on the sand, him, hovering over me—it's close, and strangely intimate. Yet he doesn't have any trouble looking me directly in the eyes.

And that is the real power of Jason King. His ability to hang in an uncomfortable situation without even blinking.

"What's that?" I ask.

"I'm going to fuck her." When he says it, he does so bluntly. Matter-of-fact. "Maybe not tonight. But I'm going to fuck her this summer. And I'm going to make her cum. Hard. And when she does, she's going to be screaming my name. Not yours."

Jason pushes back and straightens up. He flashes me a smile. "Enjoy your beer, Angel," he says before heading toward the water.

So much for Mr. Nice Guy. I hug my beer closer and nurse it.

My ears burn. I want to leave, but I'm not leaving without Kenzi, so I sip on my beer and stare off into the water. I catch glimpses of her splashing around. I try to swallow my unease, but the carbonation fizzes in my stomach and brings it back up.

6

JASON

*P*hosphorescence lights up the water as I splash in. It glows like diamonds around my hands and arms as I swim through the ocean.

The water is alive. The beach is alive.

I am alive. Kenzi is alive. We're alive, and young, and beautiful, and I want to put myself inside of her and make love to the swell of the sea.

We tread water. It's cool, but not cold. Nice.

I can hear the muffled sounds of music and laughter from the beach, but we're far enough out that we're swallowed in the dark.

She cocks her head. "Are you following me?"

"Something like that."

"Isn't Amy going to be jealous?"

"Amy isn't my girlfriend."

"Uh-huh." She doesn't look convinced. "So how many not-girlfriends do you have right now?"

I shrug. It's the only honest answer I can give.

"So what am I…the last woman on Hannsett Island that you haven't stuck your dick in?"

"I'm going to say something...and I don't want you to die of shock."

She grins. "I'll brace myself."

"I think you're pretty cool, Kenzi."

"You don't even know me."

"I know some things."

She eyes me suspiciously. "Like what?"

I rattle it off. "You're reading *Little Women*. You hate fishing. You vandalize other people's boats."

She's smiling. I like her smile. "Have you been watching me?"

I dip my chin in the water. "Sounds creepy when you say it like that."

She edges closer to me. Every now and then, I feel her toes brush against my calves, or her knees bump my legs. We're liable to get tangled, treading water like this. Even in the cool water, my blood is rushing hot.

"Do you think I'm pretty?" she asks.

There's something about the question that crushes me right in the heart. I feel my breath leave my lungs. "Yeah. I do."

"Truth or dare, Jason?"

"Dare."

Her forehead touches mine. I can feel the heat of her breath sticking to my wet skin. "I dare you to let me suck you. Right here. Right now."

My voice gets stuck in my throat. We have to keep paddling to stay afloat, and our legs brush, and I want nothing more than to be inside of her right now.

Who the hell am I to say no?

"Yeah," I say. "Okay."

She bites her lip against a smile. "See you later, stud," she says. Then she dips underneath the surface of the water, vanishing into the inky dark.

My heart pounds in my chest. I feel her fingers on the

band of my shorts, and I shift awkwardly to help her get me out of them. The anticipation of her sweet mouth has me wound tight. I glance toward the flickering light of the bonfire to make sure no one's watching us—but no. They all seem occupied, snapping open fresh beers around the bonfire.

A couple of seconds pass, and the buzz of anticipation turns into a fizzle of fear. Did the riptide sweep her out?

But then I see her—a dark figure rising from the water. She emerges on the shore, climbing to her feet.

And she has my swim shorts in her hand.

My heart sinks like a stone in the deep.

I watch as she gets on shore, stands, and then turns back to me. Her fingers curl in a wave.

I groan. "Fuck—"

7

DONOVAN

*K*enzi and I can't stop laughing as we make our escape.

"You're the worst," I tell her as I drive the golf cart back.

"Aw." Kenzi rakes her fingers through my hair. "You're the worst, too."

Jason's trunks flap in the wind, hanging off the golf cart antenna as we drive back to the marina.

It's going to be a long, naked walk back home for Jason King.

Want to find out what happens next?
  Keep reading in "Truth or Dare"!

ABOUT THE AUTHOR

The average day in the life of Adora Crooks involves sobbing about fictional characters, spoiling her nutty mutts, and watching Netflix with her beloved. Adora lives off of coffee, chocolate, and book reviews. She lives in New Orleans and daydreams about dirty romances with happy every afters.

Sign up for my newsletter to get exclusive deals on Adora Crooks stories, including ARCS and upcoming releases. XOXO.

www.adoracrooksbooks.com

Made in United States
Orlando, FL
26 April 2023

32493960R00124